Real
Ghost Stories
of Borneo 3

Real First Accounts of Ghost Encounters

By

Dr. Aammton Alias

M Content Creations

Content Pages

Dedicated to the gallant

men and women,

who are waking up

the rest of the world,

Uniting one front

onto a single realization:

together we will bring about

the ocean of change

and

to those who have failed us:

They will no longer get away.

The line has been drawn.

Acknowledgments

They say behind every successful man there is a patient and tired woman. Although I cannot profess that I am a successful man, I can definitely claim that this book and a lot of things in my life would not have been possible without my wife's constant support.   She and my studious daughter would check my stories and would be the first ones to provide me with valuable feedback.

I am most grateful and continue to be indebted to my team of first or 'alpha' readers which included my 11-year-old son, who gave honest and crucial feedback to make this book happen.

I thank the story contributors for this third book; in particular, Bob, Ariz, Amal, Yusof, Mimi, Uncle Mahmud, Aunt Lina, Farah, Desmond, Mr. Shah, Rea, Teacher Rabiatul, Syifa and Misha.   I also thank the many contributors who chose to remain anonymous.

Finally, I thank the support of my compatriots in the Reading & Literacy Association (RELA). Together we will instill the reading and writing culture amongst our people.

Introduction

Three Lines Mark the Spot

I never thought the third Real Ghost Stories of Borneo book would be this hard to write. It has been the slowest book I have ever written. I am so glad that you are reading this book as I can tell you I had a myriad of distractions and challenges that was stopping me from completing this book.

Time was a big factor as I worked most days and evenings at the clinic. I began to pity myself as I reflected upon how I had frequently talked about the importance of time-wealth compared to money wealth, and here I was finding myself in time-poverty. I would come back home late at night, finding myself tired and uninspired. My insomniac daughter was the only one who was awake to greet me whilst my wife and sons were fast asleep. I missed my sons terribly and began to fantasize pathologically on quitting and moving to a new country or alternate dimension. Eventually, I concluded I had to renegotiate my work schedule, which was to allow me to work six days a week instead of seven. In case, you are wondering; I have every Friday off, as most private clinics close on Sundays so it made sense to open when everyone else was closed.

The pressure to get this book to publication was incredible and constant. Friends, family members, and bookstores constantly enquired about when Book 3 would be out. Many had brought forward their own ghost stories which was either in complete written form, in sporadic voice notes, WhatsApp messages or shared with me in between clinic consultations. Others had sent me a few lines of text, and I had to research the area, the incident and then re-interview them. In the accounts, there were several locations I was not familiar with. I would frequently ask for 'Google Earth' snapshots to help explain their stories. I felt obliged to visit these places during lunchtime as I was not brave (or stupid) enough to venture late at night to these ghostly sites.

Here's an example of how we are using satellite images to help us with our storytelling. It actually looks comical when you read the labels and comments.

Some stories had to be edited and certain details changed to protect either the person(s) involved. In some occasions, the actual locations were not disclosed as there were concerns that the identities of the person(s) involved would be revealed.

In my last book, I had mentioned about the intention for a new theme for the third book - which was supposed to be 'travel and places'. That idea went out the window and somewhere along the line, a new theme formed on its own, which coincided with the recent climate-change movement. Can you see the theme or did I imagine all that?

Despite the challenges, producing the Real Ghost Stories of Borneo book series has brought me much joy and pride. Please consider reading the other two books.

The stories in all of the Real Ghost Stories of Borneo books are focused on ghost and supernatural encounters in the northern parts of Borneo i.e. Sabah, Brunei and Sarawak. No matter what I tried, I still don't have any (reliable) friends or contacts in Kalimantan, but that is something I am looking forward to. You will notice that the ghost sightings and experiences may differ from those in East Malaysia and elsewhere in Southeast Asia. I have some insights on why. I wonder if you have the same speculation too.

This book has had a good response with the pre-order campaign. Pre-orders made this book possible as it helped bring publishing costs down. I humbly thank you for believing in my efforts. I hope this book fulfills or beats your expectations.

As a disclaimer and precaution, I remind you that this book is not meant to encourage ghost hunting. Remember, it is important to 'be aware' and not bother them. Our worlds are meant to be separated, though, it appears that 'infractions' occur from time to time.

Once again, I thank all the contributors for their stories, and I hope you will continue to support my efforts to record more of our stories and encounters.

If you wish to share your ghost encounters and stories for the next book, please free to contact me @aammton (Instagram) and yes, all my contact details are at the back of the book. Please check the '**About The Author**' chapter.

This book was published with the help of friends and family. With pride, we pour our hearts to produce the best quality for this book. If you find any mistake(s), please accept my sincerest apologies and please let me know.

I thank you for buying this book and supporting my work, and the works of others. I hope you enjoy reading this book and all the little frights it brings you!

Abidin & The Pacer

Abidin was a 40-year-old businessman. He owned a small restaurant and had set up a managerial system, which effectively gave him more free time as he did not have to micromanage. However, his free time was quickly taken over by his extended families' needs to resolve their issues. Abidin had a very large extended family. He had so many uncles and aunts and he was thankful for that as it helped his business thrive. He realised it was time for him to give back to them.

Other than the occasional financial help, he would be asked to carry out tasks or help problem-solve his nephews' or nieces' issues. Abidin had a way with the younger generation. He never showed any judgement and he always seemed receptive to everyone's opinion.

Anyway, one day, his mother asked him to check out his Uncle Alimin's house. Uncle Alimin was a rich businessman himself. Perhaps the word tycoon was a better description. However, he had been unwell for some time. Abidin's other uncles and aunts knew very little about his happenings. He had been keeping to himself, which was unlike his other siblings. It turned out he was suffering from a poorly misunderstood auto-immune illness and he could no longer take care of himself. He had been in hospital for the past month and none of his siblings were aware of this.

It was not his only misfortune. He had recent troubles with his current wife. This was his third marriage after two very messy and public divorces. His wife had left him. Though still legally married, she was seeking a mutual separation. None of his children was staying with him and he was truly alone in the hospital.

It took a while for Uncle Alimin to swallow his pride and sought help from his siblings. In the past, when he was arrogant and full of himself, he had said some nasty things to them. He did not think he would be forgiven. Luckily for him, his siblings came to his help, without reservation and without judgement. Abidin's mother had instructed Abidin to take his cousins and nephews to go to Uncle Alimin's house.

The idea was to pack his belongings, clean the house and arrange for it to be rented out. The once affluent and powerful Uncle Alimin confided that he was broke, and his once massive savings had now been depleted. He had been so emotionally traumatised that he could not even arrange a simple rental arrangement.

Abidin was close to his cousins and nephews, though he wished he had bonded with Uncle Alimin's children. Some of Uncle Alimin's children had left the country, living with their mothers in their native countries whilst others had excommunicated with the entire family clan, a telltale sign of a very bitter relationship with their father.

Like a tasked squad, the 12 of them headed to the house compound early in the morning. The gated house, which was really a mansion by standards, was situated smack in the middle of a thriving suburb. He had built high concrete walls to surround the front part of the area, whilst the rear was facing the jungle and a small hill. By right, the mansion was fit for a celebrity or royalty, but it was in such a neglected and dilapidated state that it looked more like a haunted house or even an abandoned house in a war-torn zone. The garden and grass grew wild and gravity defying vines crept up the walls of the house.

There were at least 20 luxury cars in open garages whilst a few were left in the open, algae growing and destroying the paintwork and their tyres deflated. There was even mould thriving on the leather seats of several of the cars!

It was even worse inside the house. There was water damage in the house, from rainwater that had flooded from the balconies on the upper floor and into the carpeted upstairs lounge, destroying the designer brand carpeting. Entering the house reminded Abidin of a scene from the first Jumanji movie and he was not thrilled.

He realised it was a gargantuan task and he needed to hire professionals for the job. He didn't mind that he would have to spend quite a bit as Uncle Alimin was at one time generous to Abidin. Besides, he was not going to put his cousins and nephews through the ordeal of this massive house clean-up.

Nevertheless, everyone did their best to clean up whilst they explored the mansion. They opened doors and windows to let the sun in and more importantly, fresh air. The place stank, it had an old damp rancid smell. They also took out broken furniture and glassware that littered the floor. Clearly, there must have been wild (fit for soap tv) drama between Uncle Alimin and his estranged wife. They also tried to remove some of the foul-smelling wet mold-infested carpets.

On the upper floor, there was a set of giant wooden doors with intricate carvings which were leading to the back of the house. Abidin was trying to remember where the doors led to, but he could not recall. They tried to open the doors, but they were jammed shut. The doors were heavily rusted at the bolts. Initially, they decided to leave them alone, but Abidin could not stave off his burning curiosity. He had to see what was on the other side of the doors. With a spray can of WD-40 lubricating oil, they managed to loosen the rust from the bolts and pry open the doors. The doors creaked loudly as they opened slowly, resisting against the visitors.

Overgrown entangled green and brown vines clung and did their best to keep the doors shut as small birds flew into the house, startling everyone. With a good push, the doors flung open. The sunlight blinded everyone as they exited the dark house and onto a very spacious balcony with a large overhanging roof. The balcony was so huge and the shade providing roof was so high up enough, you could play badminton there, without any restrictions.

It was then, Abidin recalled childhood memories of having the large family gatherings and the family barbecues up there. It seemed like a lifetime ago. He recalled the view from the balcony, and so Abidin rushed across the wet and leaf strewn balcony to the balustrade edge. The view was still breathtaking and majestic; uninterrupted views of the tropical jungle and the never—ending trees standing proud and tall on the small hill.

There were several broken chairs and tables at the balcony. His nephews took them out of the house into a makeshift dumpster and searched the house for any comfortable chairs and acceptable tables. It seemed everyone was thinking the same thing. They were going to hangout and chill out here at this balcony.

An old barbecue grill was improvised and somehow, without much planning and instructions, the whole group had mobilised to set up an impromptu barbecue. One of the cousins had even gone home to bring his guitar there. Whatever apprehension everyone had was gone, and now it was the time to have fun. Of course, what was work turned out to be fun in cleaning up the balcony, sweeping up old soggy rotting brown leaves and at places, scrubbing thick layers of black algae from the mosaic tiled floor.

Abidin thought once the house was refurbished, the balcony would probably be the star attraction, making it easier to demand high rental. There was nothing more to worry, Abidin thought.

By the time they started the barbecue, it was already dusk, which was perfect timing to watch the sun sink down and be swallowed up by the earth. Cousins chatted and joked loudly, tomfoolery was rife amongst nephews and cousins, and the guitar was played throughout the evening.

The charcoal embers from the barbecue pit continued to glow as the night painted the skies black with the occasional stars. Abidin could see the supposedly full moon was partially obstructed by a large grey cloud formation.

Even so, Abidin felt an uneasiness he could not explain. He should be happy and unburdened. This house will be professionally cleaned and refurbished, and it would be easy to rent it out at good rental returns, and yet he felt a lingering mix of feelings; sadness and fear. Abidin did his best to distract himself with his cousins' and nephews' jovialness, trying his best to join the chorus of the occasional guitar serenades.

It was already late night. A few of his nephews had to go back home. It was just the seven of them left, but the so-called chill-ax party had to go on.

Without warning, boisterous laughter was interrupted by an ear-piercing cackling. Everyone had stayed quiet, baffled by who could be laughing. The cackle stopped momentarily and then continued again. It sounded un-natural, unworldly. Abidin thought the sound could not have originated from a person's throat. That was the best description he could come up with. The hair on the back of his neck stood up and he had goosebumps all over. Slowly, a few of his braver cousins walked towards the edge of the balcony. They were sure the cackling was coming from there.

They shone their flashlights at the overgrown untended garden, which seemed interwoven with the jungle vegetation.

"Anything?" Abidin asked, as he himself cautiously crept towards the balcony edge.

Nothing.

The cackling continued; this time non-stop.

An elder cousin, Ahmad, who was holding a powerful Xenon flashlight, had spotted something in the corner of the garden.

He pursed his lips in the direction, which was essentially pointing at what he was seeing with his lips. He feared if he pointed with his finger, he would provoke it. It was also a rude habit that Ahmad had picked up since he was a kid.

To everyone's horror, they saw a mysterious figure dressed in white with long black hair. Its face could not be seen. No one had to say anything, but they knew what it was i.e. a 'Pontianak' or a female vampire. They watched her 'walk' from one end corner of the garden, without trampling on or being entangled by the dense vegetation, to the other corner. Ahmad's flashlight followed her path as she glided to and fro the two corners of the garden. This went on several minutes without interruption. Abidin thought they had seen enough. It was time to leave and retreat to the safety of their own homes.

Without saying a single word, everyone nodded in agreement. Before they could move a step away from the ledge, Ahmad panicked.

"She's not there anymore!" Ahmad whispered loudly. He was really trying his best to keep his voice down, but he was bewildered by what he had seen.

This brought them back to the ledge and everyone shone their flashlights into the garden below.

"Why are we searching for it? I don't think this is a good idea, we should leave…" Abidin was interrupted by what he saw. In front of him, thick mangled long strands of hair hung down from the roof, and then the cackling restarted.

There was nothing to say, everyone was screaming and shouting as they all ran towards the doors and back into the house.

One of Abidin's cousins stumbled and fell on to the mosaic tile floor. Abidin pulled him up and they ran together towards the large doors. Before any of them could get through, the doors shut themselves closed. The seven of them tried to ram and push the large doors with their bodies, but it would not budge. Abidin's nephew; Jas, who was probably the most athletic of them, did not stop to think about their next plan of action. All he did was shout out, "Down now!" He ran towards the side of the balcony ledge and jumped over it, landing onto the ground floor, the garden. The garden where the Pontianak was first seen.

The rest of the men were shouting in panic on why he would do that, but somehow in the next 30 seconds, they knew they had to stick together and not leave Jas on his own. The Pontianak might also be there on the ground floor. Logic prevailed in the panicked atmosphere; they stood better chances when sticking together. Everyone ran towards the balcony ledge and jumped down into the garden. It was spontaneous and crazy, Abidin thought. Ahmad and Abidin knew they had to be the last two to jump down and they had to jump down together, in case of the 'last man gets captured' scenario.

They did not land softly on the soft ground. Ahmad twisted and sprained his left ankle and needed Abidin's help to hobble fast across the hostile garden. They made their way to the front gate where the others were waiting. Accounting for everyone, Abidin closed the gates and they hurriedly left the house compound, heading to Abidin's parents' house. There was no point risking any further 'misadventures' so the seven of them slept there that night.

The next day, after sharing the details of the evening incident with Abidin's parents, his mother called on her other siblings for an emergency family meeting. It was decided that the entire family clan would clean up the house that same day, along with a team of hired professional cleaners, gardeners and house repairers. The plan was to have everything ready for an evening prayer function. It was hinted that they would invite an 'imam' who was an expert in matters of 'supernatural eviction'.

Abidin was amazed at how speedily the mansion could be cleaned up and renovated by this army of professionals and his dedicated and loving relatives. However, when it was time to stay for the evening prayer function, a few of the cousins (who were involved in the balcony jump) were very reluctant. Their aunts gave them no choice but to stay. Abidin's mother would reason to them not to fear for they would fill this mansion with love again. It had not been filled with genuine love for a long time. That evening, there were no incidents and no ghostly sightings.

Within the week, house renovators came to do further repairs to the house. Uncle Alimin's siblings decided that it was better that they buy the house from him. Uncle Alimin was thankful for this as he knew he was dying. It meant that the house would continue to be within the family's possession, and not sold off by his estranged wife or claimed by any of his ex-wives.

Uncle Alimin tried his best to make amends with his estranged wife. Before he died, he left considerable and equal sums of funds to all of his children. It didn't do much to quell their hatred towards their father, as money can never ever buy love. In the 'endgame' of his life, that was the only thing that the late Uncle Alimin could do.

The mansion was never rented out; it became the family's function house. To ensure that the house was never empty, newly married members of the family was strongly encouraged - they didn't really have a choice - to stay in the mansion. There were so many rooms; every sibling of Uncle Alimin had a son or daughter who stayed there.

Abidin's mother shared with him that a house must always be filled with unconditional love, and not the endless pursuit of possessions. That is how the family clan will heal itself, and that is how the 'mansion' that has seen a lot of sadness and despair will repair its own negative energy.

Of course, from time to time, one of Abidin's nieces who lives there, can see a woman in white pacing from one corner of the garden to the other.

The Beach Resort

Fina, her fiancé Hakim and his mother Mrs. Lela wanted to have a quick weekend escapade. It was really meant to be for Fina and Hakim, but Mrs. Lela did not want any hanky-panky between the two especially when they were due to get married in several months' time. Of course, Mrs. Lela was up-to-date with modern times, she knew her son and her future daughter-in-law were 'pre-wedlock sulliers'.

Hakim also had another intention. His father died 2 years ago and he hated leaving his mother alone at home. Mrs. Lela did not want to admit it, but she had difficulty coping with her loss, especially when she was alone. Fina, whose own mother had died at an early age, had agreed that she would do her best to be there for his mother, especially when Hakim had a job that took him away from home for several days at a time. She had good relations with Fina, though Mrs. Lela did have some reservations.

It was decided that they should go to the nearby Labuan island for a few days. They had frequented this island many times before, though they would usually stay at a hotel in the town city. However, Hakim wanted to surprise the two women he loved by booking two rooms at a beach resort. He thought it was a new place, but his mother pointed out that it was actually an old beach resort that had been bought over, renovated and then rebranded. None of them had ever been to this hotel before, even when Mrs. Lela's husband was still alive.

The three of them got on a car ferry to the island and drove to the hotel. It was a beautiful beach resort, lined with coconut palm trees and with its own private beach. There was also a picturesque heart-shaped swimming pool in the centre of the resort. Fina and Hakim wondered if this would be how their honeymoon destination would be like, except they hoped it would be much further away and more exotic.

They didn't get connecting rooms, so Hakim stayed in a room which was a few rooms away, whilst his mother and Fina shared a different room. Luckily both rooms were on the same floor.

Once unpacked, they spent the day exploring the resort and then headed to the beach, where Fina and Hakim frolicked on the sun-kissed white sand beach. Of course, this was all under Mrs. Lela's gazeful watch. A part of Mrs. Lela wanted to swim or at the very least wade in the blue-green South China sea, but the comfortable lounge chair under one of the numerous straw huts proved to be too alluring. Instead, she ordered and sipped Virgin Pina Coladas, whilst the youthful lovers pranced in the shallows.

When Hakim woke up his mother, it was already sunset.

The dark orange orb had sunk into the sea, swallowed it whole and without mercy. Mrs. Lela was surprised that she had slept so well there. She wondered if she was worn-out from being on watch. Her son's and Fina's clothes were wet from swimming so they hurried to their rooms. As they were heading back to their rooms, they noticed how quiet the hotel corridor was. Fina thought it was lucky that they were on the same floor, and yet it seemed like they were the only guests in the hotel. They had not seen any other guests around. Hakim grumbled that if there were no other guests, then they should have been given connecting rooms or at least, rooms that were next to each other. Mrs. Lela insisted Hakim not to fret about it. She was keen for everyone to shower and change, and then head to the resort's restaurant and see if they can get a good 'shell-out' dining experience.

Dinner was initially a somber affair as they were clearly the only guests in the hotel. The waiters seemed nervous and unaccustomed to having dining guests. However, it was not quiet all the time. As later in the evening, the bar next to the restaurant became packed with expatriates of seemingly various nationalities mingling and dancing to the hip-grinding electronic dance music. The earth-shaking bass music was so loud, it resonated the glassware, the windows and their bodies. It felt as if they were in a party concert. The party revelers were clearly not guests at the hotel. With nothing else to do, the 3 of them went upstairs to their rooms and called it a night.

The moment Mrs. Lela and Fina went inside, they both sensed something had changed.

"Fina, do you think the staff moved the furniture? Something is very different here."

Fina shrugged; the room looked the same and yet they both had the same feeling when something had been misplaced or the furniture had been moved. The feeling lingered on even when Mrs. Lela was showering. They wondered if someone was watching them. They went to bed early in the hopes the feeling would disappear in the morning.

It was at 0302 hours that Mrs. Lela had woken up screaming. It took a while for Fina to console and calm her down. Still shivering in fear, Mrs. Lela explained she had a nightmare where a sickly young woman was sleeping next to her on the same bed. The woman was wearing a tattered black gown. In her dream, Mrs. Lela turned her head and was face-to-face with her. The woman ghost's face was horribly disfigured, the flesh was discoloured and could barely hold itself together. Her face was literally oozing out and she stank of death.

"We have to go to Hakim's room now!" Mrs. Lela insisted, her instincts were triggering all kinds of alarms within her.

Fina tried to convince her that it was just a bad dream, but she could not stop Mrs. Lela from rushing towards the door. Mrs. Lela tried to open the door. She unlocked it and yet the door would not budge, no matter how many times she tried to forcefully yank it open. Fina tried to help her, thinking it was merely her panicked state. Fina unlocked the door but she could not pull it open. It was stuck!

"Call the reception now!" Mrs. Lela shouted, as she backed away from the door. Fina picked up the room phone but the line was dead. She didn't even hear a ringing tone no matter how many times she tried to reset the phone receiver. Fina could hear something else in the silent phone. She could hear a faint sound of laboured breathing. Fina threw the entire telephone set to the floor and took out her mobile phone. Her mobile phone was not working. She could not even switch it on. Mrs. Lela tried her own mobile phone, but it was no use. Both mobile phones were as useful as bricks.

"Mrs. Lela, what's going on here?" Fina got closer to Mrs. Lela as they watched the lights in the room flickered and then dimmed. Darkness began to seep from the door, moving like it had a life of its own and quickly spread to the room.

Frantically, Fina tried to open the window. But the moment she unlocked it, to her horror, the lock moved back to its original place. The darkness crept towards the window.

There was nowhere to go so they ran to the corner of

the room and huddled together, wedging themselves between the bedside table and the wall corner. The darkness had finally surrounded them. Soon enough, the room was completely dark. They could sense there was someone or something moving around, blocking their exit.

Mrs. Lela began praying loudly in between uncontrollable sobs. Daunted, Fina feared for their lives and started reciting Holy Mantras. The darkness retreated a little. It was at this brief moment that they could barely make out an outline of a petite figure. Even though it was completely dark, they felt 'she' was staring at them with the most hostile intentions.

That night, the two women clung to each other tightly for dear life as they recited Holy Verses and prayed aloud for their protection. Horrified, they could not fall asleep. Fear kept them awake and on guard till dawn. By first light, the apparition had disappeared.

Mrs. Lela and Fina dashed out of their room and ran towards Hakim's room. Worried about his safety, they pounded on his door. To their relief, he had the usual 'disheveled early-morning look' which meant he had an undisturbed sleep.

They left the hotel the same morning, even though their rooms were paid up for one more night.

When they went back home and shared their scary

encounter with trusted family members and friends, some of them shared rumours and theories about the room and the hotel, whilst others shared their own encounters, though not as drastic as theirs. They never found a satisfactory explanation for the incident.

The incident changed the relationship between Mrs. Lela and Fina. They became much closer and she decided, with Hakim's and Fina's agreement, to push for a much sooner wedding date. Mrs. Lela convinced Fina's family that there was no need for any wedding extravaganza, as long as it was proper and legal. Hakim and Fina got married within a month in a simple but sweet wedding ceremony. They went to Langkawi island for their honeymoon, and although they brought Mrs. Lela and a very good friend of hers along, the newly-weds had their own private honeymoon suite.

Trapped

Jenny had dug her heels in that year. She knew the first year of her medical degree course at the local university was only a taste of the things to come. The first academic year was designed to get students settled in, to weed out the fake 'wannabe's whilst nurturing those who have the true passion to become medical doctors. The second year was going to be harder; they would have to study and learn faster and harder. No 'spoon-feeding education style' as common in the local high schools and colleges.

Everyone in her family looked at her like a beacon of hope. She didn't understand why. She knew there were other career paths that had better wage prospects than a medical doctor. She would be the first medical doctor in her 'family clan'. Jenny's father was a Chinese retired government teacher whilst her mother was a faithful housewife. She assumed they both wanted their eldest child to be in a very respectable profession. Sometimes, she wondered if her parents thought they lived through her, and if she did graduate as a medical doctor, it would be like they themselves became doctors. It was added pressure to her workload.

Jenny and several of her friends would spend their free time at the university library where they would go through different textbooks and journals and create their own revision notes, whilst completing their numerous assignments. They would have preferred to have joined their other friends, who were undertaking non-medical degrees; and enjoy their free time at the cinema, chill-out at cafes or let themselves loose at secret parties, but alas such was the sacrifice for the pursuit of medicine.

Jenny thought she would excel in her studies as she had no distractions in her life. However, life can be full of unpleasant surprises. Jenny never expected her father would die during this time. His sudden death was almost without warning. He woke up one early morning to get milk from the fridge to ease his 'gastric heartburn symptoms', and the next thing was he was unconscious on the floor. Her family doctor concluded that he must have had a massive 'myocardial infarction' - a fancy word for heart attack. He was supposed to have had a coronary angiogram a year ago but didn't want to distract Jenny from her studies.

She felt numb throughout the mourning period, but Jenny put on a brave face for her mother. She would only shed tears when she was alone. She tried to distract herself with med-school work, but nothing was the same. She was trapped in a numb cold world, where time passed by slowly and quickly at the same time. People she knew passed by her all the time. Many of her friends consoled her, and yet she felt she was trapped in her own bubble, unable to respond to them genuinely. She nodded when she was prompted to nod. She thanked colleagues for their condolences when she was expected to do so. She even smiled when greeted with a smile, but it wasn't real.

She would spend her free time at the university library; she would read books or do her best to appear to be reading them. Her soul was torn and she thought it could never be healed. Her same friends would join her, though she was aware they were playing more of a chaperone or minder role. They were trying to provide her with emotional support and sometimes even trying to cheer her up. She would have felt sorry for them, and yet she felt nothing. It was probably better to be in the library with them instead of going home and seeing her openly grieving mother. At least her mother could cry out to her sisters. Time was running on its own tracks; Jenny wondered when she would be able to reset, find herself again, get back to the real world and start all over.

Without warning, Jenny woke up and found herself sitting at one of the long wooden tables in the library. Thick books were strewn across the table. Her usual friends were not with her. She looked at her watch, it was 1130pm, a Thursday evening. She did not remember going into the library. She must have gone there on her own. Her friends were superstitious and would not go out late on a 'Malam Jumaat' or Thursday evening. She peered out from the corner and saw no one else there. The emptiness of the library had awakened something inside her, her instincts to survive and to escape danger. Although she was scared, she was glad because it was proof she was still alive and she was not dead anymore. She grabbed her belongings and made haste to the nearest exit.

As she walked down the long hall, Jenny could feel something was following her. She was divided on whether to look back or focus on getting to the exit. She really wanted to look back, she was burning with curiosity; but every instinct was screaming this was imminent danger. She picked up her pace, passing by the other tables faster and faster, then Jenny started to run. Halfway towards the library hall exit, she stopped, caught her breath whilst laughing at how silly she was. Assuring herself that she was being paranoid whilst in bereavement, Jenny turned back to see if there was anything behind her.

At first glimpse, she didn't recognise the dark figurine standing by one of the tables. It was slightly taller than her. Its humanoid shape was distinct black in nature, whilst its edges were blurry darkness. She saw the upper limbs were slightly too long to be human. In an instant, she realised she was not alone. Her heart was filled with terror. The lights toward that end of the library flickered and died out. Jenny screamed as an overwhelming growl filled the library. She ran as fast as she could towards the exit as the other lights in the library switched itself off, plunging the entire room into sudden darkness. She hadn't reached the exit and she was already in complete darkness. Her fiendish pursuer was getting closer and closer towards her.

Jenny reached the exit and yanked the door hard. It did not budge. It was locked! She was trapped.

Why was she locked inside the library?

Knowing there was another way out through the fire exit, Jenny turned right and sprinted across the galley of library shelves. There was no time to waste. In the darkness, she heard her pursuer crash to the exit door. Whatever it was, it was real. It was no imagination of hers. Jenny saw the fire exit sign and flung open the door. The stairs down here were dimly lit with the emergency lighting. Without any second thoughts, she jumped down, leaping over the entire flights of stairs, an impossible feat for her on any other given day.

Downstairs, the library foyer was dark. The only light emanating was from the streetlights near the glass main entrance. She dashed towards it and tried to open the door, but it was no good. It was locked. Jenny needed to break the door no matter what. She remembered there was a fire extinguisher nearby. She would use that to smash the tampered glass door. She can worry about paying for the damages later. This was live or die. She sprinted towards the fire extinguisher. It was a small one but still heavy. As she picked it up, Jenny could hear the thumping sound of heavy footsteps heading towards her. Slowly and intentionally, like an apex predator sure of its kill.

Jenny ran towards the entrance and hurled the extinguisher towards the glass door. It was a mad dash for safety. Her only salvation; break glass for freedom. The extinguisher fell short of the door and landed with a soft thud on the floor.

Not willing to give up, Jenny kicked the door several times, and tried to push and shake it open but to no avail. Jenny thought this was it, this was the end of her. With her back against the glass door and her hands ready to push away her attacker in futility, she thought about her late father and her poor anguishing mother. She wished she had seen her father's warning signs. She wished she could have diagnosed him and saved his life. It was at this moment, white lights flashed from outside to inside. It was the security guards.

She banged furiously on the glass door, and the guards fumbled through their keys to unlock the door. They finally managed to unlock the door, but it was too late. A heavy cold hand grabbed Jenny's shoulder and pulled her away from the door and into a dark corner of the library. Her limbs frantically clambered to grip anything and yet nothing. Jenny's body became colder and colder as she felt her own life being drained away from her. Her dying thoughts were wishing she was there for her mourning mother.

One of the security guards sensed there was more to a panic-stricken university student; lurched forward and ran towards Jenny whilst reciting a mantra. He grabbed her hard and yanked her out of the building. The other security guard slammed the glass door shut and locked it, as the other guard and Jenny rushed to the safety of the grass patio. Still trembling, Jenny found herself sobbing uncontrollably.

The security guards didn't bother to re-enter the library building. Once Jenny had calmed down, they told her not to worry as they would go in after dawn and clean up if there was a mess or any damages inside. It was many weeks later that they told Jenny that they had suspected there was a supernatural being in the building, appearing and preying on the emotionally or spiritually weak.

After that incident, Jenny spent more time at home with her mother. She opened up to her; cried together and eventually laughed together as they shared the fond memories of the man they loved. She thought this was the first time she had truly bonded with her mother. She stopped trying to be someone she wasn't. When times were hard, she opened up to her mother and her best friends, and when they themselves needed emotional support, she made sure she was there for them too. She did well in her studies and eventually graduated with her friends.

The Construction Site

Before I became a Muslim convert or the correct term would be, Muslim revert, my name was Chong and I used to work for a construction company. We were mainly involved in building and civil works projects. Those in my industry would say we learnt best on-site. Truer words were never spoken.

In 2005, we were awarded a government project to construct a multi-storey building with its surrounding facilities. Make no mistake; we fought tooth-and-nail to win this contract tender. It was a do-or-die situation as at that time, the country was going through an economic recession. Construction companies were scrambling to win any construction contracts so as to keep their heads above water, doing their best to keep ahead of their debts. 'Ride out the tide and hang on until things get better'. During this time, many construction companies went belly up, adding themselves to ever-increasing list of bankrupt and failed companies.

Winning the contract meant that we had work and we did not have to shut down the company, but it was no golden egg. The project we were awarded was worth $8 million. The management had to price itself over-competitively as they were not sure how long the recession would last. Essentially, the two-year construction project was done at a loss of $450,000, provided there were no further surprises. The economy was that bad. In order to survive we had to take a loss. It was important that the company remained functioning, and its employees continued to have jobs to do.

There were the three of us who were tasked to manage the construction project at the site-office. The project was located at an old public dumping ground in the Capital. I remembered when I was still a child back in the 1970s, this was the place where stray dogs were kept before being 'put down'.

We had the area cleared and leveled. A 'portacabin-style' office and plywood temporary housing for around 100 labourers were built in record time. Our labour workforce was an international mix of Thai, Indonesian, Indian, Bangladeshi, Vietnamese and Malaysian Murut. Each nationality group had built their own quarters, but they all mingled well as one big family. They had been with the company for many years then.

Work was arduous, I frequently worked till late and many times I had to stay in until the next day. There was no choice as our boss had to reduce our site-office operating costs, which meant I only had one part-time office administrator for support.

Every evening, I would head back to the site-office and work away on my computer. I had to finish reports, draft letters and perform data entry so as to chart and monitor the project teams' daily productivity. We had an extensive work programme which needed constant reviewing and assessment. With this data, we could plan for the next work component. At that time, it seemed like a never-ending job; but as the teams completed the different sections and work goals, it gave us all a sense of fulfillment.

I had been so absorbed in work, that I did not notice how fast time flew. I would only notice the time when it was near midnight. This was when everything was really, really quiet and then there was a small disturbance interrupting the silent night. I started hearing and noticing the unexplained. I had never believed in the 'unseen' or supernatural. At that time, I believed that everything could be explained by science. Initially, it was easy to dismiss the so-called unexplained.

In the beginning, I had noticed subtle 'signs'. My office room was facing towards the front of the site-office. I had a clear window which overlooked the meeting room. The pantry was on the left of the meeting room. From the pantry, there was a door that led to the walkway leading to the toilets. In my office, I had an exhaust fan built into the wall a few feet above where I sat. It blew air towards the toilets. This was useful as I was a heavy smoker back then. It kept my room less smoky.

When it was past midnight, I would usually hear creaking noises. It sounded like either footsteps on the wooden floor inside the locked office or at times, it sounded as though it was coming from the outside walkway leading to the toilets. I thought it was the workers who were using the toilet or having a cigarette outside the office. However, when I peeked out from the backdoor, I would find an empty corridor which was overlooking the dark jungle. The labourers' quarters were a good 50 metres away. Not a single soul in sight. I would sometimes peek through the exhaust fan in the hopes to catch someone, but nothing.

There was also the frequent creaking noise inside the office. What's with that? I could never figure it out. I theorised that must be because the office was made from wood timber and the air-conditioner made the office cold and that somehow caused changes as the outside of the office was warm. Of course, I was not a scientist. What did I know?

In addition to that, I started noticing shadows frequently zipping past the window in front of me. I was all alone in my office, and all the doors of the site-office were locked. I triple-checked all the doors were locked for security reasons. Thefts were common in the area. I reasoned that perhaps I saw those shadows because it was late and my eyes were fatigued from looking at the computer screen all night long. Whenever I looked up from reading hardcopy reports, I would catch the occasional shadows passing by quickly. I was very tired. I reasoned that it must have been my mind playing tricks on me.

Sometimes, I would make visiting rounds at the

labourers' quarters during the day-time and late evenings. It was easier to do the rounds during late evenings, before I head home for the night. I had to check the welfare of our labourer employees.

I noticed that whenever I did the night rounds, the workers would always warn me not to go to specific areas. These were the areas which were nearest to the jungle. I told them I had to because I had to inspect their housekeeping and cleanliness. Nevertheless, I did my best to respect them and would inspect the areas in the morning instead. I never bothered to ask them why.

The site-office disturbances went on for a year, but it did not bother me too much as the construction project was progressing well. However, something different happened one unfortunate evening. I was working late again. I was actually expecting to work through the night until the morning so as to prepare for a progress meeting that very morning.

At around 2am, there were loud creaking noises out in the back. It was much louder than before. I made my way cautiously to the back; a heavy 'Maglite' flashlight in one hand and then I yanked the door open. I had to be prepared in case of an intruder. But nothing. There was no one there. It was the same old routine. I decided that it was time to break routine.

I yelled out asking who it was. If once wasn't enough, I yelled out for a second time, but there was no answer. I felt a bit foolish because if it had been an intruder, he would surely not answer. Anyway, I closed and locked the door and went back into my office. I heard the same noises later on, but this time, I chose to ignore it. Work must come first.

By 3am, I had looked up and saw a dark figure standing by the window. I thought I saw a face with red eyes, but it seemed so blurry I could not really tell what I was looking at. It moved away from the window and I could hear footsteps. That's the intruder, I thought.

I jumped out of my chair, same flashlight in hand, and ran into the meeting room. I am an above average built guy and I was pretty sure I could take down a burglar. And yet, there was no one there. The meeting room was brightly lit. In fact, all the other rooms had the lights on too. I was sure there was someone there. I had goosebumps all over me, but I refused to be spooked out. I went out of the site-office and headed to the security shed. The security guards told me that they did not see anyone in the area. They all gave me an odd look. I ignored them and went back into the office. Work must come first. It was like the entire office was busy with fast moving loud shadow-like people, but I was determined to finish my work and I ignored everything else.

After the sun rose to a new morning, I felt unwell. My eyes were burning dry. By late afternoon, my eyes were so painful that I had to go to the hospital. The examining doctor told me that I had a complication of severe conjunctivitis. I was actually hospitalised for 2 weeks! Who on earth would ever get hospitalised for conjunctivitis? The specialist doctors thought it was a very serious complication though. Up to this day, I still don't really know what it was. When I got discharged from hospital, my eyes were still red but less painful. It took me another 3 weeks to completely recover.

Work had to come first so as soon as I was discharged, I was already back on my feet at the construction site. The good thing was that most of the work for the building was done and I did not have to stay overnight in the site-office. Eventually, the building complex was completed in time and it was certified safe for use.

Much later on, I did find out why the labourers did not want me to inspect the specific areas of their quarters in the middle of the night. There were fearful of the spirits that were frequently seen there. The workers had numerous encounters with the supernatural. They saw dark tall figures jumping at long distances between treetops, and it was surely no monkey. Some saw an army of faceless shadow-like giant figures or 'Orang Tinggi'. Others saw 'Pontianaks' or the female vampires from time to time, whilst other saw different forms of the Bunian spirits. I am grateful that I have not had such an encounter.

Of course, those days are long gone now. I no longer work as a construction contractor. I joined a Government

Linked Company (GLC) and my years of experience has helped me advise others in my office-based job. I took up the name of Yusof and much has changed about my life i.e. less drama, less stress and yet better fulfillment and most importantly, tranquility.

The Neighbourhood

Amal had shared and written a few stories with me. She had previously shared with me a story titled "A Father's Daughter - which can be found in the second book: Real Ghost Stories of Borneo 2.

***

My siblings and I were pretty much used to seeing spirits here and there. I could feel their presence even if they did not reveal themselves. However, I had never let them bother me. I was never spooked by any 'presence'.

After I had gotten married, which was 5 years ago, I seemed to have lost that ability. I was no longer sensing or seeing any spirit beings, which was good as it helped me focus on my life with my Eurasian husband.

About a year ago, things changed. My husband got an amazing offer to buy a house in the city. It was too good to think twice about, the location was central, and everything was near it i.e. highway, the airport, the Mall and the mosque. He looked at the house and saw it was beautiful and could not believe it was unsold for a year, and at that price, he thought he wouldn't need to consult his wife! It would be a pleasant surprise, he thought. He signed the papers and came home to tell me the good news.

I was very shocked at how easy it was for him to make such a big decision. A man should not buy a house without consulting his wife first. I had expected a joint decision. I did not want to dampen his jovial mood as he had always mentioned buying our first house would be a life milestone for him. As much as I tried to warm to the idea, I felt something was wrong. My female intuition was warning me that there was much more to this house and that I had to be ready.

The house was located in a cul-de-sac that seemed invisible from the main road. The vegetation and the way the trees had been planted had been intentional to make the entry road inconspicuous. I could not believe this amazing location. This neighbourhood had appeared out of nowhere. Mature gentle tall trees surrounded both sides of the driveway.

The house itself was a semi-detached house with a beautiful front-yard garden. Its pearl white paint was flawless, which meant it had been newly painted. Flowers of every shape and every colour grew in the garden; clearly the work of a dedicated gardener.

What a beautiful house! I can't believe it hadn't been sold for over a year. I thought to myself. My husband was expecting me to say the words, tell him that he had made the right decision. I wanted to say so but decided to keep my emotions to myself, until I had made a full assessment of the property.

It was only when we first stepped into the house that I had felt it. To describe this sensation would be like a winter cold gale that had blown straight at me, bone-chilling coldness seeping into me, making it hard for me to breath as my chest tightened. It was exactly like the first time I had an encounter with a spirit being.

It had been a long time since I had felt their presence, and it was all such a shock to me. I thought I would never feel them again.

My husband could tell something had changed within me.

"Do you want to go home now?"

"No, let's see this through." We had a quick tour of the rooms of the house. I would always look back to see if there was someone behind me. I knew 'it' was watching us. I had hoped that by looking back, I would keep the spirit in check.

I noted that even though the house was listed as unfurnished, some of the furniture had been left behind, including the bed in the master bedroom. I could only conclude that the previous owner was not given 'permission' to remove the furniture by the spirit of the house. When we stepped out of the house and hurried to our car, it was then I realised all but one of the houses in the neighborhood looked like they had been vacant for some time. A house across ours got my attention. I could see a little pale girl with dark eyes staring at us. I quickly looked down and told my husband to drive off immediately. I kept my head down, whilst reciting 'protection verses'. I was on the verge of tears; everything was coming back to me. I wanted to be normal again.

Once back in the safety of our parents' house, I told my husband about what I had sensed. He was initially skeptical. He was never sure what to make of my special gift when I told him a long time ago, before we had gotten married. However, when I went through the logic of how such a beautiful house, located in a strategic location was unsold for over a year and that he got a wonderful bargain for it, he agreed that it must have meant that the real estate agent had not disclosed entirely everything.

For the next few days, we mulled about what to do. The right thing would have been to sell it off, but then, it would be irresponsible to pass the house to an unwitting buyer. In the end, we decided to have the house 'cleansed'. Besides, it would be amazing to live in such a house. If, and only if, we could evict the resident spirit(s).

My mother had suggested a man who was well versed with the Holy Book. He was supposed to be a specialist in cleansing houses of spirits. My husband would always refer to this person as 'The House Cleanser' which sounded funny, even though it was quite a serious matter. The House Cleanser could also verify if there were occupants in the house and not just something I had misread. I had also brought my mother along with me. Like myself, she was also gifted. She could see the spirits most of the time.

When we brought him to the neighbourhood, he knew this was their ground. We had not told him much about the house, but he said there was something wrong with the house and he went on to explain why it had not been sold for such a long time. We never told him that. He said the house had not been occupied by people for at least 5 years! The real estate agent must have lied to us - he told my husband it had not been sold for just over a year.

The moment we stepped into the house, I felt a strong and malicious presence, this time it was much stronger than the first time I had visited the house. Our Cleanser man told us to leave and stay outside the house. He would walk around the house and find the occupants himself.

The first thing he did was to go into the master bedroom. There he saw an entity appearing as a woman in a white dress, lying down on the bed. The moment he entered the room, she stared at him with her dark black eyes. When he didn't leave and started reciting Holy Verses, she screeched hysterically at him. We could hear this awful sound from outside the house. My husband could not believe what he was hearing, it was a terrifying sound, unnatural and not of this world. All of the stray dogs around the neighbourhood ran towards the house and began to bark. The three of us huddled together in fear.

We heard the sound of several people running inside the house. It sounded like they were running from the master bedroom to another bedroom.

After a while, the House Cleanser man opened the door and asked my mother and I to come in. He wanted my husband to stay put, but my husband insisted on joining us. The House Cleanser told my husband to keep an open mind and not to utter a single word whilst in the house. He knew my husband had a hard time believing in the supernatural.

I was hoping it was all over. I was hoping the House Cleanser had come to show the house had been cleared but it was only the beginning. The House Cleanser told us that I had to tell the 'woman of the house' that my husband and I would be living in this house from now on and she cannot stay here.

Why me? I thought this was crazy. Am I really going to evict this spirit from my house?

Every step sounded off a loud creak as we cautiously climbed up the staircase. I could feel my heart pounding hard and fast against my chest. Near the top of the stairs, the House Cleanser told us to stay put for a while. He began to chant Holy Verses. As he was doing so, there was a blood curdling scream, followed by whimpering. My instinct was to run downstairs, run out of the house, go back home and never set foot here again. The House Cleanser told us not to leave. "No, don't. You can't let her know you're afraid of her. This is your house and you need to let her know that she cannot stay here."

I could tell my husband had difficulty in accepting the situation. He could not see anything, but he definitely felt an evil presence nearby.

The House Cleanser gestured with his hand to follow him. I was to stand immediately behind him. He opened the door to the master bedroom. It was very cold, colder than before. Our breaths gave out mist even though it was a hot tropical morning. In the corner, I could see a lady in a white dress with her back towards us. She had dark black hair that flowed all the way to the floor, and it swayed on its own from right to left and then back again. I was so scared she would turn around, reveal her face and then start attacking us.

I joined the House Cleanser in reciting Holy Verses; my mother and husband also recited with us.

After that, whilst shivering in my shoes, I mustered the courage and told the lady in white, "You can go wherever the hell you want but you cannot stay here. This is our home now and if you do not move, then we will destroy you."

I heard the lady wailing loudly, and then without warning, she began to cackle sickly. I stepped behind the House Cleanser in case of any unpleasant surprises. The four of us slowly stepped back and closed the door.

We went to all the other upstairs bedrooms and recited Holy Verses inside each of the bedrooms. In the last bedroom, I could see what appeared to be children with unkempt long hair, dressed in raggedy and dirty white robes - their backs turned against us; their dirty hands with long fingernails tapping against the wall. I asked the House Cleanser if I had to say anything. He told me that there was no need, as they would listen to their mother. We recited Holy Verses here as well and then left the bedroom, closing the door slowly. My mother and I could hear crying as we left that room.

The House Cleanser told us that the downstairs room were already 'cleared'. He advised us to wait at least 40 days before moving in. I should have asked why does it have to be 40 days. Why can't it be sooner? But the whole ordeal had drained me.

When we got back to the safety of our parents' house, my mother and I talked about what we saw i.e. the lady in white and, we assumed, her children. My husband said he could not see anything. The rooms were empty, but he could definitely sense some form of danger, an ominous presence. He had a hard time accepting what he had experienced.

A week later, we had gotten in touch of the caretaker for the area. We were impressed by how well he had taken care of the area. In fact, the caretaker did all the gardening and landscaping for all the houses in that cul-de-sac. Interestingly enough, he told my husband and I that he knew about the lady in white who had been staying in our new home.

After 40 days, we came back with the movers, and began moving our belongings into our new house. The caretaker told us the other 'occupants' had moved out. I was very happy to hear that.

I thought it was all over.

Every time I stepped out of the house; I had felt uncomfortable. I had a feeling that people were watching me. But not from inside the house, but from outside the house.

I looked at the vacant house in front of our house. Upstairs by the window where I had seen the little pale girl on the first day; well this time, I saw her. The little pale girl with the dark eyes. She wasn't alone. Standing next to her was the lady in white with dark black eyes, and three little boys with long unkempt hair. They looked very sad. I uttered a prayer, begging for protection for my husband and myself and I said sorry for taking their home, but it was our home now. When I looked at the window of the house opposite ours, I did not see anyone or anything there.

Sometimes, I could feel them watching us from the other house. On some nights, I get the occasional knocking of the window in the master bedroom. I would try my best to ignore it and went back to sleep. On the advice of my mother, I placed Holy prayer books at all our windows, which apparently is not a rare practice in this country.

In time, I grew used to the idea of our 'neighbours' watching us. I did my best not to provoke them and hope and pray that they won't hold an everlasting grudge against my family.

Adam & The Waterfall

How did I meet Adam? I had finished work and realised I had a business question to ask Johnny, a good friend of mine. He asked me to join him for dinner at his Kota Batu house. He mentioned his brother was cooking, and he was a good cook. His brother Adam was a Chinese Muslim convert. When I first met Adam, Adam was keen to share about his life experience. Immediately, I knew that my mentor's mentor and his mentor are the same person. Gobsmacked I realised that my meeting him was no coincidence. It was of 'divine' significance. And indeed, it was a strange evening and an even stranger conversation. We stayed up all night, whilst Johnny - whom I had intended to talk to - fell asleep by the dining table.

Before Adam converted to Islam, he had many, many adventures. Of course, his adventures did not stop after he converted but it was less 'daring'. You see, Adam was always looking for strange things. Magical things. Perhaps he was looking for proof of God. He wondered if he could witness magic or something beyond science, then it would prove the existence of God.

Anyway, about 25 years ago, Adam was a successful Chinese businessman. Being wealthy, he would travel a lot, especially around the region. This was the time when he started collecting bizarre mystical items. During that time, he was married to a woman who was living in Kuching city. This gave him an opportunity to spend a lot of time on his own exploring the tropical rainforest of Sarawak. He was yearning for something, but he was not sure what it was. Perhaps it was the same lure of the rainforest and tribespeople that brought the likes of Bruno Manser to Sarawak.

One day, Adam had heard about a magical waterfall deep in the jungle. He was told that a spirit princess lived there. The waterfall was located somewhere near Mount Singai and Bau Village. Adam tried to find a local guide and porter to bring him and his supplies, but most were reluctant to go there, no matter how much money he offered them.

"Are you crazy or what?!" was their standard response. Eventually, Adam decided he had to put his foot down with the next guide he was going to negotiate with. Anyway, he offered that the guide didn't have to stay at the waterfall with him. He was to be picked up in a few days' time.

The guide was so shocked with the request, "Do you have a death-wish or what?" The guide explained that the spirit princess at the waterfall had been known to kill unwanted visitors. Adam forked out a wad of cash to shut the guide up, which was more than triple the going-rate. To make sure the guide would come back after a few days, Adam told the guide that he would pay half upfront and the rest would be paid when he picks him up. They shook hands on the agreement, and then bought and packed supplies for a week.

The trek through the jungle to the waterfall was not easy. There was no pathway or jungle track through. The porter and Adam had to slash a path through the thick foliage. It took them two days to get to the waterfall.

They reached the waterfall around noon time. The sight was spectacular; a paradise waterfall, falling from so high up, it looked like it was pouring from the heavens, way above the jungle tree canopy. Curtains of white water rushing down, hitting the irregular rock surface and breaking into more and more white curtains of falling water, crashing down into a small lake-river below. Large round flat pebbles littered all around the waterfall. The sound of water was so intense, it would drown out all melancholic thoughts.

The porter wanted to set up camp towards the jungle edge, in case of 'flash' floods but Adam insisted on wanting to be as close as possible to the waterfall without getting wet. The porter tried to get Adam as close to the jungle edge, whilst Adam insisted to be closer to the waterfall. After much negotiating, Adam got his campsite set about 2 meters away from the damp pebbles area. He got his fire started too.

Before leaving, the guide asked Adam, "Are you sure you want to camp here alone?"

"Don't worry about me. The money is waiting for you here too," Adam reassured the guide. He thought he heard the guide utter to himself, "I'll only get the money if you don't get killed…"

Adam thought the guide was so negative about the area. He brushed it off and congratulated himself for finding such a magical and beautiful waterfall. He took off his clothes and went skinny-dipping in the river.

Later, he caught himself a medium sized fish, an Empurau, which is quite a rare delicacy. He cooked the fish at the campfire and thought about his luck in life, how he had everything in life i.e. health and wealth and yet he felt somewhat empty. At least here at the waterfall, he was truly a King in his own mini-kingdom.

After the meal was done, Adam laid in his sleeping bag in his tent. His tent was essentially a see-through mosquito netting. The idea was that he could gaze at the stars all night long. In the darkness of the jungle, there was no light pollution which meant the stars of the galaxies would twinkle in the night sky. It was a majestic view. Here there was no one but him. The rainforest night critters would buzz loudly and yet almost orchestrally and harmoniously. Almost.

Of course, if it started to rain, he could easily get up and install the tarpaulin over the tent structure.

Adam didn't know when he fell asleep, but he was woken up abruptly. He looked up and it was dark and silent, other than the constant roaring of the waterfall. The stars had gone from the night sky and was replaced by a black canvas. Yet, something was not right. Where had all the stars gone? Still lying in his tent, he grabbed his flashlight and pointed it towards the sky. When the light reached skyward, he saw there was something overwhelming above him.

A giant dark creature with maggots crawling from its body. He pointed the light immediately above his head and saw the creature's face. It was a hideous woman-like face with long hair that flowed over the mosquito tent and onto the ground. She had four kitchen-knife-size sharp teeth, whilst the rest of her teeth were oddly shaped and crooked.

Adam gasped in terror; his sleeping bag was immediately soaked with his sweat as he trembled in fear, his flashlight still focused on the demon's face. His every instinct was to jump up and run towards the jungle, away from this demon and away from the waterfall. And yet deep inside, Adam knew this was a matter of life and death. He knew that if he ran into the jungle, he would be a dead man. Even if the demon creature didn't chase him, he would end up lost forever in the jungle and die from exhaustion. His instincts told him that if he was going to die, it would be better to die there on the spot, in his sleeping bag!

He trusted his instinct, switched off the flashlight and covered his head with the sleeping bag and pretended to sleep! Of course, he could not sleep, he was so scared he wet himself. The demon started growling and then let out a heinous cackle. Adam did not budge. He had to take his chances in his wet sleeping bag. He waited and waited for the demon creature to attack him, and nothing happened. After several hours, Adam fell asleep and woke up late in the morning.

After washing and drying his sleeping bag, Adam realised he would not be picked up until 3 days' time!

He was stuck there in this killer paradise. He decided to make the best of it. He did his routine, keeping himself to the pebbled banks of the waterfall lake, swimming and bathing under the waterfall. If he was going to die, this was the best place to die at.

Before nightfall, he caught another Empurau fish and cooked it by the campfire. The delicious fish helped him forget about his worry about the night. He had a plan. He was going to sleep early and stay under the still damp sleeping bag, ensuring his head was completely covered under the sleeping bag. If it worked the night before, surely it would work tonight as well. At least that was what he thought.

After washing his cooking utensils in the lake, Adam could hear a high-pitched womanly voice singing. The singing pierced through the roaring waterfall and echoed throughout the area. He could not understand the words that was being sung, but she sounded so melodious and yet sad. He looked around to see where it was coming from. Something had caught his eye, a glint or two, emerging from the rock surface of the waterfall. He stood frozen as he saw the silhouette of a woman in black, floating through the waterfall. The water and the water spray did not touch her; as the waterfall parted to let her through. She hovered inches above the water and then floated towards him. Her long hair, which reached to her feet moved on its own - it covered most of her face, except for her shiny black eyes like ominous polished beads and her evil grin, revealing a set of fine sharp teeth. This time her teeth were of 'normal size'. This did not reassure Adam. He ran towards the safety of his see-through tent, dropping his cooking utensils.

Adam took no more than a few steps and something grabbed his foot. He fell on the ground head first and blacked out. That night, he dreamt of meeting face-to-face with the floating woman in black at the waterfall. She snarled at him and told him to enjoy the last day of his life. She sunk her claws into his body repeatedly as he groaned in pain.

Adam woke up early morning. His head was sore, and he could feel the large bruise on his forehead. His body ached everywhere. As he nursed his bruised forehead, he saw his arms and chest had small round punch-out bruises. Adam felt very weak as he remembered the events of last night and the ensuing dream. He staggered to his sleeping bag and fell asleep in the hot humid day. He slept so soundly and only woke up in the middle of the night. He was dying of thirst, so he got up and gulped down his bottle of water. He needed more water and there was only one way to do that. He started his campfire and walked to the waterfall lake to collect water. He added some purifying tablets inside his bottle before capping it off. Almost expectantly, he saw the outline of the lady in black in the waterfall. He was filled with fear, and then something unexpected happened. He was overwhelmed with rage as the lady in black floated towards him, with her long hair covering most of her face but her dark shiny black eyes and her evil grin with the sharpest rows of teeth. He shouted at her, "Stop it! I am not afraid of you!" He dropped his water bottle and picked up a large pebble and threw it at her. The pebble went through her. She moved faster towards him, but he was angrier than scared and he stood his ground. As she got to an arm's length from him, he started throwing punches at her.

"Calm down, Adam!" A voice emanated from the lady in black and yet he did not see her lips move. Her grin seemed permanent.

"How do you know my name?" He was baffled; he stopped trying to punch her.

"I know many things. You should not be here. Go home." The lady in black continued.

"I am looking for something. Maybe you can help me." Adam had to ask.

"What you seek for, the answer is not here, not in my waterfall. The answers you seek for are closer to home. You need to know the questions first before you can start seeking the answers."

"What do you mean by that?"

The lady in black remained quiet and then slowly floated back into the waterfall.

"WHAT DO YOU MEAN BY THAT?!" Adam screamed out to the waterfall. He was hoping the lady in black would re-emerge but nothing. In anger, he started throwing pebbles at the waterfall. He didn't care for the cost of his provocation; he was yelling for the lady in black to come out. Eventually, he got tired and sat by the waterfall lake edge and waited for as long as he could until he dozed off on the pebble banks.

The next morning, Adam woke up grumpily. His back was aching everywhere. After a good swim, he had a siesta. In the late afternoon, Adam was woken up by the porter. The porter had been worried about Adam and arrived a day earlier. They packed their gear and headed back to civilization. Adam offered no information about his encounters and the porter did not bother to ask him about his experience. They didn't talk much until they got out of the jungle and back to Bau village.

When Adam paid and thanked the porter, the porter asked Adam if he found what he was looking for.

Adam could not hide his disappointment, he shrugged, "Who knows…"

It was almost 20 years later that Adam realised the questions to the answers he was looking for. This all happened near his home, and not somewhere deep in the jungle. He embraced Islam immediately after that.

The Blue Lakes

Junaidi and his wife had just started moving to the new national housing scheme area at Lugu Village. The national housing scheme was basically an affordable housing project set up by the government to allow its citizens to purchase cheap and yet decent built houses interest-free. It was considered to be one of their great personal milestones, house ownership.

To drive to their house, they would have to drive pass by a man-made lake at the bottom of a hill. The housing construction company had used the clay soil here to top up and elevate the surrounding plain, where the houses were to be built. They had dug a hole so deep and large that rainwater started to collect. The water was so clear you could see the bottom of the lake, and best of all, the lake had a light blue hue to it. Hence, the lake was frequently referred to as The Blue Lake of Lugu.

Even before Junaidi found out he had been granted the house at Lugu Village, he had always desired to snorkel and dive in the lake. He was very much inspired by a free-diver named Justin (you can check his YouTube video). He tried to convince his best friend, Jus, to explore the lake. However, Jus was a 'spiritually connected' friend and he told Junaidi that the lake had a 'penunggu' or a powerful spirit dweller. No matter how many times Junaidi tried to convince his best friend, Jus would always say bad things would happen if they went there. Junaidi thought that was all rubbish superstition. Of course, when Junaidi started moving to the new house, he kept nagging for Jus to swim and dive into the lake, but to no avail. Interestingly, he heard a few of his co-workers mentioned the same thing. Junaldi brushed it off believing it was a deterrent urban myth meant to keep children from swimming and consequently drowning there. After all, if Justin the famous free-diver survived snorkeling and free-diving there, then it should be pretty safe from 'spirits'.

Anyway, Junaidi and his wife decided to move their belongings piecemeal into their own cars. They would pack as much as they could and then drive to their new house after work. When they arrive, they would start cleaning, dreaming about and debating on their ever-changing plans for the interior design of the house. Then they would drive home late at night. They could have simply hired movers and transported everything over a period of a few days, but they concluded that this would be their last house-move. No more moving after this - they would settle down here and grow old together in this house. They chose to cherish moving their belongings to this new place. It would be a slow and hassle-free move. Whilst they packed up and unpacked their precious belongings, they would reminisce about the memories associated with each of their belongings in between sips of their evening tea and coffee and the ambience of nostalgic songs. With the children at their grandparents, it was the rekindling of middle-age romance.

One evening, Junaidi and his wife lost track of time as they got carried away with their unpacking activities. Part of them wanted to sleep over the night there at their new house, but since the bed wasn't there yet, it meant roughing it out on a few bean bags. However, even at 2am, the children were still waiting to be picked up from their grandparents'. They got into their SUV and slowly drove out of the housing suburb. Most of the houses there were vacant and dark. It seemed others were taking their time to move into the houses, perhaps waiting for interior renovation or (illegal) external construction work. Junaidi's wife held his forearm harder. Instinctually, he knew what this meant. She must have seen something that spooked her. His wife was known to be able to see the unseen; as much as Junaidi loved his wife, he was skeptical about her 'sixth sense'. At 2am in the morning, Junaidi was wondering if he was feeling or sensing something sinister in his surroundings. Driving slowly through the rows of empty houses, Junaidi was relieved to see the exit road.

As they neared the exit, Junaidi saw a long thick shimmering black rope on the asphalt road. It looked quite peculiar; the way the rope coiled a few times on itself. The rope appeared to be thicker than Junaidi's forearm, in fact, it reminded him of the giant long ropes used on oil tankers and ocean-crossing ships. The rope moved on its own as the car approached it! One end of the rope stood on its own, raising itself to a height above the hood of their SUV. Both Junaidi and his wife could see two almond-shaped crimson red and yellow lights emanating from the end of the rope.

There was no doubt in their minds that this was a giant snake and yet, the car light did not reveal the snake's body, light simply vanished from the edges of the snake's body. Its eyes glowed an unnatural red with a streak of yellow against the headlight beams. Mesmerised and dumbstruck, Junaidi did not react fast enough to brake the car. Their car ran over the giant snake!

"Was that really a snake?" Junaidi quivered as his wife nodded and trembled.

He set the car to reverse mode, which activated the rear-view camera. There was no way he was getting out of the car in middle of the dead night, especially with that giant snake out there.

"Junaidi, what are you doing?"

"Making sure it's not under the car!"

The snake was still coiled, its head was raised high up - it started to level to the rear window. It was poised ready to strike the rear of the car. He had expected the snake to be dead, but it wasn't. Junaidi's heart started to race, wondering if it could break the tampered glass windows.

His mind raced wildly on how such a huge snake would appear here of all places.

Junaidi's fear was overwhelmed by rage. Rage consumed all reasonable thoughts, which was to drive away. He slammed the accelerator which pushed the car backwards and the car ran over the snake again. They felt the bump hump of the wheels going over the giant snake, and then he drove forwards. Junaidi put the car in reverse and thru the rear-view camera, the snake rose and coiled up, defiant.

"No, you bloody don't!"

Junaidi pushed the pedal to the metal and propelled the car backwards, running over the snake, and then slamming the brakes. His wife screamed in horror. Junaidi shifted the auto gear and revved the car forward. The car lunged forward and then he slammed the brakes.

"I am gonna kill whatever you are!"

He did this several times; until his wife yelled and begged for him to stop. "Please Jun, this is crazy. We don't do this in the middle of the night. Please, what if it isn't a snake…"

As his wife began to pray loudly, Junaidi changed the auto-gear stick to reverse again and looked at the screen. He could see the snake was still up but this time, it started to slither towards the kerb and headed towards the grass.

"One for the road!" Junaidi yelled out fervently as he reversed the car again to run over the snake, but this time, he missed. From the safety of their car, they looked around to see if the snake was on the grass, but nothing. The snake was nowhere to be seen.

"Junaidi, don't ever do that again! That is just complete madness." Junaidi stayed quiet as he realised the snake was headed towards the direction of the blue lake. The lake was dangerous after all. As he drove home, he had so many questions in his mind, like how did the snake survive his car rampage and more importantly, why did the snake retreat? Was it because it had enough of his car or was it the prayers his wife was chanting?

Junaidi had trouble sleeping that night. He started to regret trying to kill the snake. Eventually, he did fall asleep, but it was not a pleasant sleep. He kept on waking up from time to time; he had a feeling someone or something was in his room watching him. He would recite a prayer verse and try to go back to sleep, but the feeling was still lingering.

Since it was a Friday morning, Junaidi and his wife decided to move more belongings in the morning and went back to their current home by late afternoon. They were not going to go back home late night as a precaution.

As Junaidi drove towards their new house, he drove pass by the blue lake of Lugu. He could see a bare-chested dark-skinned boy sitting by the banks of the lake. He was soaking wet; he must have had a swim. He looked like he was around 7 to 9 years old and he was alone. He was looking towards the edge of the lake and yet his eyes were staring at Junaidi's. Junaidi thought it was dangerous for children to be swimming alone, especially when there could be a snake at the lake.

"What a stupid kid and what irresponsible parents!" Junaidi uttered out loudly.

His wife glanced her window, "What are you talking about?"

"Did you see that child who was swimming by the lake? Scandalous, I tell you. Parents need to be aware of where their children are, at all times."

His wife could not see the boy, and wondered what Junaidi was talking about.

"It can't be a ghost, okay. It's daytime and the hot sun is out. I saw a kid, so come on, don't let last night's incident spook you out!"

His wife said no more. They unpacked everything and started rearranging the furniture. It seemed like a futile exercise as everything would have to be rearranged when they bring the main furniture.

Soon enough, it was half-past noon, which was time to head to the mosque for Friday prayers. Junaidi had to drive past the same lake. He quickly glanced and saw no child or any oddities there.

"Not a ghost," he reassured himself.

After Friday prayers, Junaidi drove again pass the same lake to get to his new house. There, he saw the same child sitting by the lake bank, wet and shirtless. His eyes were vacantly staring into the distance. Junaidi slowed his car to a snail's pace. He wanted to tell off the kid but just as he was about to roll down his window, the child raised his left hand, whilst still staring away, pointing to him. Junaidi felt a bone-chilling sensation run down his spine. He quickly drove off and later on, he started to laugh to himself, "There's no way that was a ghost. Ghosts don't appear in broad daylight. I can't believe I am such a gullible fool."

When he got to his new house, he saw his parents-in-laws' car was parked in the garage too. They had come to inspect the house. He suspected his wife must have told them about the snake incident, so they were to 'spiritually inspect' the house too.

Over coffee and 'tea tarik', Junaidi shared about his concerns about this solitary child swimmer at the lake. His mother-in-law nearly choked on her tea.

"How do you know it's not a spirit?" she asked.

"It's day-time," Junaidi reassured her.

"The spirits or 'Penunggu' can appear at any time, not just night-time. Besides, don't you find it strange that this so-called child is swimming on a searing hot morning and afternoon, and on his own?" his mother-in-law shook her head, "I have no doubt that was the Penunggu at the lake and I think it is very much related to the creature you tried to kill last night. Junaidi, what were you thinking? You are a family man now, you have responsibilities."

Junaidi felt like he was being scolded by his mother-in-law. After that day, Junaidi avoided driving pass the blue lake. If he had to drive past the lake, he would make sure he was not alone and more importantly, he was not driving late at night. Every time he neared the lake, the hairs on his forearms would straighten up, and he could see the same boy there waiting at the lake banks, to which he would do his best not to look at.

A month later, a famous blogger wrote about the 'Blue Lake of Lugu' and after that, the lake became quite a popular spot to swim or lounge by. The locals started setting up wooden stalls to sell food and other goods, whilst others started standup board paddling there. There were even a few ladies who decided to pose in their bikinis for a swim and photoshoot, which caused a social media uproar. Once the lake became popular, Junaidi could not see the mystery boy spirit anymore, even when he tried his best to search for him (without getting out of the car, of course). Thanks to rampant human activity, the blue lake slowly turned dark green; the water was no longer crystal clear, and the bottom of the lake was no longer as visible from the surface.

To compound matters, a devastating jungle fire; likely set by a smoker hiker, had burnt down the trees and vegetation protecting the hill, and lead to soil erosion into the lake. There was enough black burnt soot, wood and soil that was washed into the lake. The trees were an important part in protecting the lake and now there were gone.

Junaidi concluded that as much as spirits can be terrifying, Man was the true monster; destroying everything he touches. He wondered where the spirit boy had gone to. Was he tired of Man? Was he scared because there were so many people visiting and having fun at the lake? Too many people to scare at one time, perhaps?

He wasn't looking for trouble; but he wanted to know if the spirit boy had truly disappeared or died. Perhaps it was not a ghost after all. He wondered if it was a real boy after all. Did he drown? Did his parents scold him for swimming there? He kept doubting himself. Junaidi found excuses to explore the hill by the lake. It was accessible especially since fire destroyed much of the inaccessible shrubs. He would climb to the top of the hill and find the view breath-taking. He would see the rows of white and orange houses and the little people, like ants, who were busy with their lives. He realised that even though this was his neighbourhood, he knew nothing about his neighbours. He was disconnected with them, and everyone there lived disconnected lives. It was at that moment he realised how silly he was trying to connect with a spirit boy. With time, Junaidi forgot about his blue lake resident.

***

One day, Junaidi decided to explore the surrounding area. He took his young sons and they hiked through the small gentle hills near the Lasuk road area. He took with him a metal walking-hiking stick. It was fun to climb up the orange-clay rich hills with his sons. It was a good bonding time for him and his sons, exploring the nearby unknown.

Once they got to the top of one of the hills, they could see the entire suburb of rows of neatly arranged houses. Junaidi saw a winding path that led down to the other side of the hill. Junaidi wondered where it led to. They walked down the winding path, jumping over small gullies and other interesting weathered erosion landscape. When they reached the bottom of the hill, Junaidi and his sons were confronted with a surreal view of a still mirror-like blue water lake. Although it was a bright day, the light was dimmer; there was more shade cover from all the dark and creepy trees surrounding the lake, the hills and the surrounding path. It was a breathtaking sight and yet, there was creepiness about the place that Junaidi could not explain.

He noticed the lake seemed very shallow in the middle. He could see muddied footprint tracks running from the bank, into the shallow lake bottom and to the other side of the lake. Junaidi unreasonably thought his sons and himself could walk across this shallow part of the lake to reach to the other side. The more he thought how 'safe' the route seemed, the greater was his temptation to cross the lake. Common sense should have dictated that crossing this lake was dangerous. Something was messing with his mind. The more Junaidi realised this, the more he could sense a sinister supernatural being was nearby.

Not wanting to feel daunted, Junaidi decided to challenge whatever 'presence' he was feeling. He shouted out to the lake, "I am not afraid, I am Man, conqueror of this world!" He laughed out loud, realising how silly it sounded. He heard echoing of his voice, but all he could hear from across the silent blue lake was the echoing of "Conqueror of this world," - none of the words he said before that and none of his laughter.

As he turned his back away from the lake, he saw the silhouette of a black humanoid figure standing by one of the large trees. Instinctively, he sensed it was no human. He had goosebumps all over his body. His sons did not notice anything but from their facial expressions, he could tell they were worried about their father's restlessness.

Junaidi remembered about the spirit boy he had previously encountered. He was wondering if it was the same spirit. There was something very different about this entity. It looked taller and more menacing than the boy spirit. There was no doubt this place had a much stronger Presence than the old blue lake. Junaidi came to a realisation that this was not a place to take risks. Fearing for the safety of his sons and himself, they headed back up the hill. Junaidi heard loud sloshing in the water and felt a primordial sense of danger. Something was chasing them.

"Run, run till you get home!" He shouted to his two sons to run for their lives, "Don't look back, just run home!" He made sure his sons ran up the hill where the path to the main road could be seen. His sons wanted to check on their father, but Junaidi pushed them on, "Don't think about me, get safe, get home!"

They jumped over a small gully. Junaidi tripped and fell. "Go on, don't stop!" He beckoned his sons who were already half-way up the hill, As Junaidi got back on his feet, his whole body fell backwards. He felt his pursuer was behind him. He got back on his feet and jumped across the small gully. It was a jump for freedom. No, it was a jump for his dear life.

He was stopped half-way across the gully, and in mid-air, his entire self was thrown backwards. He landed on his front and hit his head and face. Struggling to get up, Junaidi clambered on, trying to get up. A vice grip around his ankles stopped him from getting away. He could barely stay awake; he could feel his own life being extinguished. His vision turned blurry and all he could see was light and darkness. He heard his own words echoing around him, "Conqueror of this world." A giant shadow figure approached him, and everything faded to black.

Junaidi was awaken by vigorous shaking and light-slapping on the face. It was his wife. She was in tears and hugged him tightly when he woke up. She helped him get back onto his feet and then helped him hobble up the hill and on to the main road, where her car was parked. The short car ride to their house was silent, other than the sobbing of his wife and his youngest son.

A few days later, they decided to talk about the incident. Junaidi's wife told him that her mother had called. Junaidi's mother-in-law was panic-stricken. She had a premonition that Junaidi and his sons were in immediate danger. Junaidi's wife got in her car and saw their sons on the main road. Putting her children in the safety of her car, she ran up the hill and down the winding path where she saw Junaidi being slowly pulled down the rocky path before the small gully. She saw a dark mysterious demonic figure near Junaidi. She chanted a prayer whilst begging 'it' to let her husband go. The demon faded into thin air and she rushed to save Junaidi.

They never ventured to the area again. Junaidi and his wife are always wary of isolated and quiet blue lakes.

Interestingly, Jus told him that there were several other clear blue lakes in the area, one of which an uncle of his, had witnessed flying Pontianaks, but that is a story for a different time.

The Lugu blue lake – now a bit green.
Courtesy of Google Earth

The hidden blue lake – Lasuk Road blue lake.
Courtesy of Google Earth

This photo taken from a vantage point is only possible after a recent jungle fire. The water is actually light blue.

Mahmud & The Police Housing

My uncle Mahmud is a well-respected recently retired police officer. Every time I mentioned to a police officer that he's my uncle, I seemed to gain access to a whole different attitude. It was clear that he was a good police officer; he was smart enough not to get involved in the politics of work and more importantly, he carried his good character values with him during duty, off-duty and now during retirement. I have always bumped into him walking with his smart and beautiful wife (yes, Auntie, I am super-praising you!) at the local malls, and even in the neighbouring country. I would joke with him, and say "Hey Uncle, you are retired now, you got no right to follow me around!" Him and his wife lead what seem to be a simple life with their grown children, and they spend their time travelling regionally. One day, I decided that since I have bumped into them too many times, I ought to stop my so-called busy life, sit down and have a good chat with them over coffee.

They would ask me about my dual life i.e. being a family doctor and an author and somehow, I always ended up asking them if they have had any ghost encounters…

It was the 1990s, when life seemed to flow abundantly; at least on the surface it seemed to do so. Mahmud, a graduate police officer was made detective. Everything in his life was picking up; his work and family life. He had just gotten married with an awesome Chinese lady who had started out her career as a science teacher.

As glorious as it may sound, Detective Mahmud's job was arduous and painstakingly difficult. He had to deal with difficult people and people in difficulty whilst the working hours were long and unpredictable. The nation's people who were not accustomed to reporting crimes and incidents to the police and would previously prefer to deal matters in their own hands, began to seek out police help and police involvement. Expectations ran high. Of course, expectations would usually lead to disappointments.

Detective Mahmud did his best to keep his spirits up, being humble and supportive to his fellow officers and underlings, whilst listening with good intent to the parties in difficulties.

As part of his work experience rotation, Mahmud was transferred to the Belait district. The Belait district, is known as the oil-mining district, is situated on the other end of the tiny nation. Nevertheless, it was still a good 4 to 5 hours' drive each way, since the national highway was not yet completed. It did not make sense for him to commute daily, especially when he had out-of-office-hours duties. He was hence given accommodation at the Panaga (village) Police station compound. His wife Lina would stay there too, and she managed to get a temporary teaching job there.

Panaga village or just simply known as Panaga was significant to the nation. The national oil and gas exploration company had built its headquarters here, which also meant that there were a significant number of expatriates living there.

The Panaga Police station compound was beyond a complete set up. It had accommodation barracks with officer quarters, a mess hall, a mosque and of course the Police station itself. The Seria river flowed around the edge of the police garrison; which in many ways was like a defensive moat. There was also a large lagoon-like pond there.

When Mahmud and Lina arrived, they noticed the mature jungle trees fronted the Southern perimeter. Their accommodation was allocated near the centre of the compound. It was a semi-detached house structure that looked quite regimental. Mahmud immediately noticed that the house structure had no visible bricks; it was likely to be made using pour-in concrete, which was a technology developed in the 1950s. At that time, it was revolutionary but now it looks obsolete and too rigid. They were not put off by the aesthetics, as the interior was spacious for the two of them and their Filipino house maid or amah, Mary.

They moved their few belongings to their new dwellings and went out to shop for groceries. After a quick dinner, they settled in for their first night. Mahmud was to start work early tomorrow morning.

Sometime in the middle of the night, Lina; who was sleeping snuggly in their cool bed, was suddenly awoken by very loud crying. It was so loud that both her husband and her jumped out of bed. They had no doubt that it was the sound of a baby crying; almost screaming in their ears. There was no baby around in their bedroom and yet it was as though the baby was there. They heard rustling in the living room and the sound of furniture being kicked. Grabbing a police baton, Mahmud ran into the living room and flicked on the lights. His wife had followed behind him, armed with a small metallic alarm clock. The alarm clock was the nearest thing she could grab in defence.

The crying of the phantom baby had suddenly stopped. The lights revealed Mary in her pajamas and bewildered, in the middle of the living room. From the looks of the overturned coffee table, they deduced that their housemaid had ran out of her room and tripped over the coffee table in the dark.

Mary confessed she had panicked and ran out of her bedroom when she heard the loud crying. She thought the eerie sound was coming from right next to her left ear. It was at that moment Mahmud and Lina realised their maid was correct. The loud crying was coming from right next to their ears!

He looked at his watch and saw it was 0102hours. He sighed and concluded he needed a resolution to this situation. Mahmud sat down on one of the sofas and recited a prayer, and after he was done, he reassured everyone that everything would be alright. Mary refused to go back into her bedroom and decided to sleep on the sofa in the living room.

The rest of their sleep was uneventful. Mahmud had to get to work early, whilst Lina stayed in bed a bit longer. Later in the morning, after a hearty breakfast, Lina decided to check out her garden and more importantly, find out if their neighbour had heard anything.

Salmah, their neighbour, was a bit surprised when she met Lina. Salmah's husband was also a police officer but she did not know exactly what his post was other than he was being paid well, worked longer hours than most policemen and he never ever talked about work. Lina asked if she or anyone in her household had heard a baby crying the night before.

"Oh, not again! I thought that was gone already."

Lina was startled by that response, "What do you mean again?"

"The previous resident there had complained about the same thing but we never heard any babies crying. And all of my children are very much grown up."

Lina was not particularly superstitious, but she was shaken by the thought. Salmah tried to console her, "Don't worry about it! If the sound is loud, it means the entity is far away. It is when the sound is not so loud and seemingly distant that you should be worried, because it would mean 'it' is very near."

Lina thought that did not make sense. However, she chose not to talk about it anymore. She did not want to give away how worried she was about staying in the compound. When she got back to the house, she busied herself in unpacking and sprucing up the house along with Mary.

She cooked dinner for Mahmud and waited for him to return. The dinner she had cooked had turned cold by the time Mahmud rang the home telephone. Mahmud was going to be very late that evening. In fact, he was not sure what time he would arrive home - he had an emergency night duty. Lina did her best to hide her disappointment and wondered if this was the life of a police officer's wife. Lina decided to turn in early.

Sleeping soundly, Lina was awoken again by the loud crying of a baby. This time she was aware the sound is emanating from near her left ear! She looked around in panic and there was no visible sign of danger. She covered her ears, but the sound did not disappear. She ran into the living room, which was dimly lit, and saw Mary was fast asleep on the sofa. She assumed Mary could not hear the same eerily disturbing sound. She poked Mary to wake her up, but it was clear Mary was deep in slumberland. Perhaps she had taken a sleeping pill, Lina wondered.

It was at that moment, Lina realised she was all alone in that house, with the sound of the crying baby in her ears.

In anger, Lina shouted out, "I am not afraid of ghosts!"

The disturbance immediately disappeared. Lina looked at the wall clock. It was 2 minutes past 1 in the morning. Mahmud was still at work, and she was left to her own devices. Before she could dwell on her new realities, the front windows of the house shook. Lina raced in fright to her bedroom. She searched for Mahmud's police baton. Running back to the living room where Mary was dead asleep, Lina could make out odd-demonic shapes. There were dark humanoid silhouettes dashing to and fro across the drawn curtains. She heard loud rustling and marching of several loud footsteps.

"I am not afraid of any of you!" Lina turned to the one emotion she knew could help her to overwhelm her fear: rage.

Undaunted, Lina flung open the house door, gripping the baton so tight she could barely feel her fingers. She was poised, ready to attack those who chose to confront her peace and her new home. As she stepped outside of the house, long shadows swayed aggressively on the patio and porch. The pavement light flickered its orange light and dimmed. An army of shadow emerged from the darkness. A fleeting thought of retreat was squashed by the realisation that it was all too late. This was do-or-die, though she thought it was more of do-and-die! The horde of darkness came closer to her and she found her breathing shallow, and her chest tight. Her limbs grew heavy and she found it harder and harder to keep the police truncheon, her only means of defense, held up high above her shoulders. The shadow demons had gotten much closer that she could have leapt forward and struck them. If only she had the courage. Much of her rage dissipated whilst a sense of hopelessness and defeat began to creep in.

Before she could do anything else, her wrist was held tightly in a tight grip. She tried to resist, doing her best to free her arm from her attackers. Having failed that, she screamed in terror.

"What are you doing?" It was a familiar voice. Mahmud's. Lina felt safe again, cried in her new-found solace and embraced him tightly.

Once back inside their house, they noticed Mary was still fast asleep on the sofa and unaware of the recent happenings. Lina explained that she was tired of the disturbance and she was going to attack the ghost or ghosts. She simply could not accept that her life should be dictated by whatever 'Presence'. Mahmud was very upset about her reasoning and actions, because he thought that any experience with a ghost was far better than an encounter with a person who may have bad intentions. Leaving the safety of the house in the middle of the night was never a wise decision, even if they did live in the middle of the police garrison compound.

Since that night, nothing else strange happened. With time, Lina found out that the Panaga police station had a significant history. It was the only police station that held out against heavy and ferocious attacks by Indonesian-backed rebel forces in the 1962 rebellion. Other than the possibly bullet-proof pour-in concrete walls and the Seria river that naturally surrounded and protected the compound from being over-run, the brave police officers in 1962 fought valiantly against rebel forces, to protect the Sultanate and their very families who lived with them in the compound.

Even now, from time to time, Lina wonders if the baby crying and the 1962 hold-out against the rebels were related.

The Feline Incident

Manisah, a nurse graduate, had shared an incident that happened to her father a long time ago.

Sometime in the year 2002, Manisah, who was eleven years old at that time, was staying in a wooden stilted house on the mangrove muddy banks of the river at Sungai Matan Village. Her parents along with her shared the house with her two aunts, who themselves had their own families.

It was an old yet sturdy large stilted house; there was more than enough space for everyone. Her grandparents had actually moved to a brick and mortar house higher up the riverbank, on dry land. Her grandfather actually gave the house to his eldest son but he himself had already built his own house in the suburb, so he got his younger brother i.e. Manisah's father, to live there with their two sisters. That way the mangrove-wood house would not be left vacant. Her grandfather had built a wooden walkway that connected the modern house to the stilted house so that way, they could walk to their grandparents' house and onto the main road without getting their feet wet.

They had a peculiar setting. There was another stilted house in front of theirs. There used to be a connected wooden walkway between the two houses, but a dispute upset their grandfather and he demolished his part of the walkway. The neighbours had been throwing rubbish into the river and no matter how many times they were advised not to do so, they persisted even to this very day.

Manisah's grandparents were very upset as their neighbours' plastic rubbish would accumulate at the riverbank, and eventually, the swans which would usually flock and wade near their house stopped visiting altogether. That was the last straw for her grandfather. The adults no longer talked to each other; even during festivities, they did not visit each other's houses. They pretended the other did not exist, though Manisah and her neighbour's children would play together around the area. Even the children did not talk about the problems of the adults. As long as everybody minded their own business, there was peace.

Unlike typical 'Kampong Ayer' or water village residents, neither Manisah's families nor the neighbours had 'perahu' or wooden boats and they were not involved in the nation's favourite pastime i.e. fishing. No one ventured down into the river or on to the brackish muddy mangrove flats. Their world was connected to everything on solid dry land: motorcars and tall concrete buildings.

Manisah thought this was normal for her. The only thing that crossed both her family's and her neighbours territories without any issues were the cats. Both families had a dozen or so cats, although no one was really sure who owned which cats. Actually, it was more likely that the cats themselves decided which member of either family it owned! The cats had free rein on where and when to stay. They marked their territories with their solid and liquid excrements. With ample food from both masters (or slaves - whichever perspective you take), they bred well, sometimes a bit too well.

One of the female cats that Manisah was fond off had given birth in a thick cardboard box next to the shoe rack outside the main door and somehow Manisah ended up being the caretaker for the cat's new litter. She would take care not to appear too interested in the tiny newborn kittens, in case the mother cat decided to reject any of the kittens.

The kittens grew as their black, white and orange fur grew thicker and they were starting to crawl within their box. Days later after that, the kittens were already starting to do their best to explore the edges of their box. It was not long after, that they tried to claw their way out of the box.

With a bribe of pasteurised cow's milk and moist cat food, Manisah would lure the mother cat out of the box after the kittens had their breastmilk. As the mother cat chowed down the cat food and licked the milk, Manisah would play with the kittens in their box. She stroked their tiny bodies and their thin fur. This went on until the kittens were about a month old. The mother cat had gotten accustomed with Manisah, plus later, Manisah had found out she was an empath which meant cats and other animals would naturally seek her, as though they were trying to communicate with her.

Manisah had come back from afternoon school and rushed to the balcony where next to the shoe rack, she greeted her kittens with glee. However, she became alarmed. She checked again and counted four and not five kittens. The only orange kitten was missing.

She searched the cloth and rags inside the box but there was no trace of it. She looked inside the nearby shoe rack and peeked inside each and every shoe but the fifth orange kitten was nowhere to be found. She hadn't even given it a name and it was already gone. Manisah wept uncontrollably.

It was at this moment she heard a very faint crying. It was coming from below the house. It was definitely a kitten's cry. She peered down, below the house and into the river. She could see the orange kitten was clinging for life onto one of the house stilts. The kitten was wet, it must have gotten out of the box and gone through the balustrade railing and fallen into the river. It was getting dark and the tide was coming in. Manisah tried to encourage the kitten to climb up further, but it refused. It was already shivering whilst clinging onto the wood pillar.

There was only one thing to do - she would go down to

the riverbank and wade through the water to rescue the kitten. It was going to be dangerous as it was getting dark, but Manisah didn't care.

Luckily, her father caught her as she was running across the wooden walkway to their grandfather's house. After explaining her grand rescue plan, Manisah's father scolded her and instructed her to go inside the house immediately. 11-year-old girls have no right playing or rescuing kittens around Maghrib time, he reasoned. He would go and rescue the kitten himself.

Manisah's father, Jiman, was no brave man. In fact, most people see him as very cautious and very superstitious. Some might say Jiman was a big coward. In most circumstances, he would have let the kitten drown. The circle of life, he could argue but he loved his daughter and he would hate to see her heartbroken if the kitten drowned.

Against better judgement, he found himself going down to the riverbank using the makeshift ladder which was placed in the middle of the walkway. He had not been down on the riverbank for many years. The sun was setting, reflecting dark orange-amber light and long black shadows on the surface of the river. The house lights barely lit the surrounding area.

Jiman waded slowly towards the house pillar where the orange kitten was still meowing for help. He was wearing thick sandals and that did not protect him from the pain of stepping on the numerous hard mangrove tree shoots that were all over the river bank. He had to navigate through the never-ending flotsam of plastic bags and other plastic rubbish, which seem to float towards him. He began to loathe his inconsiderate neighbours.

As he neared the pillar, Jiman had an all too familiar feeling that he was being watched by a 'Presence'. The water was already upper thigh deep. He really wanted to leave the kitten, and at the same time, he realised he was so near. Jiman recited a mantra as he grabbed the wet shivering kitten and placed it in his breast pocket.

"You owe me so much, you silly kitten!" He muttered under his breath. Jiman was feeling tired and the water was unexpectedly cold. He turned around and began wading back towards dry land.

"Who?" A deep voice echoed behind and then all around him.

In instinct, he glanced back and saw a dark shadow-like figure behind the pillar where he had rescued the kitten earlier. Panicking, he picked up his pace wading across the water. How he regretted looking back! He should not have seen it. He could have pretended he didn't hear anything. Jiman could hear loud splashing behind him. It must be chasing him! Nearly stumbling into the water, Jiman neared the dry riverbank, he fought against the heaviness of his legs and the resistance of the water. He was moments away to safety, he thought.

An apparition, in the form of a rather pale lady in a white tattered robe appeared on the dry riverbank in front of him! She had dark sunken angry eyes and long black hair that reached her ankles. Jiman choked, as he thought he was now trapped between land and river. Bringing his gaze down so as not to stare at the lady ghost which was clearly a 'Pontianak', he turned right and made a mad dash to dry land, avoiding the Pontianak. As his heart palpitated out of his chest, he sprinted up a small mound towards a chicken coop which was situated next to his father's house.

The last time he had run this fast was probably during the 50-metres dash in high school. As he caught his breath at the small chicken coop, he realised his feet and slippers have been cut by the mangrove shoots and roots. He started to feel the burning pain of the small cuts.

Jiman tried to act calm and cool, he didn't want Manisah's grandfather to laugh at him for being such a coward when encountering the supernatural. Jiman's father i.e. Manisah's grandfather, was a different kind of man. He was very outspoken and frequently abrupt. He was also known to 'put the ghosts in their place' i.e. he could challenge a Presence directly and somehow, they would behave and disappear. Jiman was a completely different man. He was quiet, non-confrontational and soft spoken, and everyone knew he was no brave man.

He checked on the orange kitten in his breast pocket. It was meowing gently and doing its best to snuggle in the warmth of his pocket.

"Don't worry, you are safe now. I will get you back to Manisah," Jiman whispered to the cat.

He walked towards the back of his father's house, but it was all locked up and dark. The only light that was on was the white fluorescent light outside the back-patio door and the lights in the living room, which was basically a security precaution. Jiman then remembered that his parents had gone to his eldest brother's house for a dinner function.

He had to make his way back to the makeshift ladder that would lead him back up to the wooden walkway to his house. He dreaded the idea; it meant he had to go halfway down towards the riverbank. As he walked past a banana tree, Jiman saw the same lady ghost, the Pontianak, staring angrily at him. He veered course, and without thinking much about it he ran a wide S-pattern path, in the hopes of confusing the Pontianak of his intended destination i.e. the ladder. He could hear a distorted wailing sound immediately behind him. The sound got louder and louder. Whatever was behind was getting closer and closer to him.

As Jiman reached near the ladder, he performed a near Olympic feat, i.e. a long and high jump from such a distance and landed halfway up the ladder. A searing pain jolted into this right shin, but he persevered and pulled himself up the ladder. Without stopping, he dashed across the wooden walkway to his house. Banging the wooden house door frantically, his wife only had to open it slightly and he pushed the door hard and jumped onto the living room floor, whilst protecting the orange kitten in his pocket with his left hand. Landing with a loud thud on the wooden floor alarmed the residents of the house.

Blood was all over on the laminate floor, oozing non-stop from his right shin. When Jiman saw the blood and then the large wound on his lower leg, he screamed in pain. His sisters and their husbands rushed to help. They compressed and stopped the bleeding and later cleaned the wound.

When everything and everyone had calmed down, Jiman passed the orange kitten to Manisah. The mother cat was very happy to see its kitten again. That made Manisah joyful and proud of her brave father.

Jiman's leg wound did get infected and he had to see a doctor for a round of antibiotics and sterile dressings. He thought he must have injured himself when he jumped on to the ladder. His doctor thought he was lucky not to have fractured his bone. His elder sister had a different opinion though - she believed the Pontianak had struck him. Nevertheless, the antibiotics must have worked as his leg wound had healed.

A few days later, Manisah's father installed chicken wire at the balustrades so that the small kittens would not accidentally fall down into the river. He was pretty sure the next time a kitten falls down into the river, he would let it drown.

Somehow, Manisah's grandfather found out what had happened. He told Jiman that; no matter what, a kitten's life is never worth the risk of going into the river. He revealed to Jiman that there was a reason why no one in their family worked in the river, why none of their family members go out fishing or 'me-rambat' in the river. The exact reason was never disclosed to Manisah. Manisah believed it must be something like a curse or a jinx, but even to this day, she does not really know the exact details. Unlike other river houses, their family house does not have stairs or ladders that go directly from their house into the river.

As for her orange kitten, the kitten grew up to become seemingly fond of the river. It occasionally swims in the river.

The Tattoo

I have mentioned Zul's ghostly encounters a few times already, as these stories were narrated by my mentor Bob, and later on, by Zul himself. However, the actual first story was something I had first decided not to write about as I was unsure of what to make of it. As I got to know more ghost encounters from other people, I realised that at least one other person had a similar encounter as Zul's.

Zul lives in a large house near Junjungan village. He has 5 siblings and they all live in the same house. Zul's eldest sister, Julia, was 19 years old then and had one of these sticky relationships with a policeman from a nearby village. They had been together for a few years now and their relationship never seemed to wane. They went everywhere together, constantly text messaging, phoning and video-calling each other. When they went out together, they would sit or walk so close to each other as though attempting to defy the borders of unacceptable PDA in this society. Of course, when the adults weren't around, they would hold hands and cuddle each other tightly. The parents of this young policeman wanted a speedy engagement and marriage, but Julia's parents disagreed. It was important for Julia to graduate with a bachelor's degree from the local university. They would have preferred if she would work for a few years before actually settling down.

However, Julia and her beau could not accept this, so they had gotten formally engaged with the plan of getting married immediately after graduation. Sometimes, Zul felt overwhelmed with the mushiness of their relationship and promised himself that when he grows up and has his own girlfriend, he would not be such a pathetic dope like his sister and her fiancé.

One of the things that the family found annoying was their almost 24-hour video-calls. It did not run up their mobile phone bills because they would connect their mobiles through the house Wi-Fi. This meant everyone else may have slower internet download rates. Julia was the eldest sibling so essentially amongst the siblings, she was the boss, and no one could tell her to stop video-calling.

One evening, Julia felt a bit insecure in her room. She didn't want to be left alone and yet she had to finish her assignment. Her room was the best place to finish her work, away from her rowdy siblings. Julia would have preferred to be accompanied, so instead she video-called her fiancé whilst leaving her door open.

During this video call, they each set their mobile phones on a holder so that they could carry out their own work, whilst occasionally checking on each other and had short conversations. It was multi-tasking at its finest.

With the peace of mind, Julia focused on her work, whilst her fiancé worked on his own police report.

In the meantime, Zul had come back from a football game and was climbing upstairs to his own room. Julia's room was near the stairs and Zul could see her sister's door ajar. As he walked pass by, he peeked into his sister's room. He could see a silhouette of a person behind his sister who was sitting by her table. Zul thought Julia's fiancé was getting more audacious by coming into her bedroom. Leaving the room door open whilst he was there was still unacceptable. Zul's parents would be extremely upset if they knew, Zul thought. "They better get married quickly, it's getting quite annoying," Zul said to himself. He really wanted to say something but realised his place in the family. Zul walked away and went to his own room.

As Zul showered, he wondered about the person in his sister's room. The person seemed a bit too tall to be his future brother-in-law.

Later on, Zul walked slowly towards his sister's room. He slowly peeked from the side of the door. He could see that his sister was busy working on her assignment.

"Who is that by the door?" A familiar yet diminished voice came from inside.

Julia turned around and caught the peeping tom.

"What are you doing, Zul?"

"Just checking on you, 'Kaka'. I will close the door and leave you as you are." 'Kaka' was the title he had to address his eldest sister by, which literally meant big sister.

"No, please leave the door open, Zul."

"Yes, Zul, listen to your Kaka." The same voice. Zul could see it was coming from Julia's mobile phone, a blurred video image of his future brother-in-law.

Zul nodded, went downstairs for dinner and then played a video-game on his PS4 console.

Near midnight, Julia got tired and rested in bed. She didn't want to sleep alone so she asked her fiancé to leave the video-call 'channel' on.

Zul was also tired so he went upstairs. He tried his best not to steal a peek into his sister's room, but somewhat he could not help himself. He took a quick glance and saw his sister was on her bed. He saw her arm was across her chest and caressing her neck. Something bothered him about that, but Zul kept walking on. He didn't want his sister to label him a peeping tom.

Zul laid down in his own bed and thought about the image that was bothering him. Julia's arm seemed strange, she must have been wearing a strange lace pattern on her arm. He thought he saw symbols on her arm.

Restless, Zul, who had quite an artistic talent, got up, took pencil to paper and drew the pattern or symbols from memory.

By the time he had finished, he realised it wasn't a lace pattern. Before he could think of anything else, Zul's mobile phone put a stop to his train of thought. It was Julia's fiancé. He sounded distressed, he wanted Zul to check on Julia immediately.

Zul ran to his sister's room. It was for a glimpse of a moment. Zul could barely see a dark figure sitting on Julia's bed. The only thing he could see, without a doubt, was its slender yet deformed hand on her neck, and he saw its long arms had gothic-looking symbols and patterns tattooed on it. Julia was choking in her sleep.

Without thinking much, Zul jumped towards the figure, fists poised ready to strike the creature. With the blink of an eye, the intruder had disappeared into thin air. Zul woke his sister up, who was screaming and gasping for air. The whole household was woken up with that scream and they rushed to Julia's room. The danger had already disappeared, leaving Julia confused and sobbing uncontrollably in tears.

Minutes later, her fiancé came around to the house to check on Julia. Her fiancé had seen that there was someone else in her room. Although he could not see the figure clearly, he could see its long pale arms.

That evening, Julia's parents allowed her fiancé to sleepover, on the one condition that everyone (yes, everyone) slept in the living room.

After performing a prayer ceremony, Julia's parents consulted an elderly lady who was well-versed in matters of spirituality and the spirits.

It was not revealed to Zul what exactly had transpired but he thought he overheard his parents talking about Julia's fiancé having a jealous suitor. Whatever the reason was, the incident pushed Julia's parents to get their daughter married as soon as possible. Julia and her fiancé had to promise that she had to graduate with flying colours, which was really her parents telling them not to get pregnant until she has graduated!

A few years later, without realising it, Zul had turned his drawing of the pattern-symbol tattoo into one of his art displays at school. His brother-in-law had gone around to check on Zul's art exhibition.

When he saw the pattern-symbol, his brother-in-law stared frozen at it. He told Zul that he recognised the 'tattoo' he saw on the arms of Julia's mysterious attacker. Zul took the drawing down for fear it would bring misfortune. He showed it to his uncle, 'Bob' who immediately recognised the pattern; it was a tattoo signifying the spirit belonging to a clan that was a harbinger of great suffering.

Nikki & The Staff-house

I had met Nikki whilst working at an on-site clinic for one of the construction consortium companies who was undertaking the largest construction project in the country. Nikki, a Filipino nurse, had been working for the company for the past 5 years. Although she missed home, she was always surrounded by other Filipinos. In fact, she shared the same accommodation as the other Filipinos in the company.

Nikki decided to tell me her strange experience at this staff-house in Pintu Malim village.

The company needed to rent a house near the construction site. An old but large rectangular house was found in Pintu Malim village, and it was literally next to the construction site. The house was really meant for a large family as it had ten large rooms. The view from the house was splendid as you could see the river from the front and you had the jungle and hill view at the back of the house. There was also a large abandoned backyard which had several trees including rambutan fruit trees growing fruitfully. However, this house had not been rented for the past 10 years, and the owner offered such a low rental for the house with ten rooms, a mere $500 for a large house. Of course, the company was expected to pay for the renovation of the house, to convert it into a suitable staff-house.

The men stayed in the rooms downstairs, whilst the female staff were given the upstairs rooms. There was a hallway that connected all the rooms upstairs and unlike the downstairs room, each room had their own bathrooms en-suite. The men had to share the downstairs bathroom and shower rooms. The women were quiet about this arrangement as it was a luxury to have been considered by their company. As a security arrangement, there was a double lock on the main door on the upstairs floor. There was only one entrance and exit which was this main door.

When Nikki had first moved in, she was allocated in one of the rooms at the end which faced the river. She was sharing the room with two other Filipino female staff. Nikki chose to have the bed that was closest to the en-suite bathroom - shower. This meant she would be the first to shower in the morning, at least that was what she had hoped for.

Nikki had not had any trouble staying in the room. The three ladies would come back after work and share their daily happenings and more importantly about the things they missed most in the Philippines. Nikki began to notice subtle things which disappeared when she became inquisitive. For example, she sometimes caught something in the corner of her eye. She could not tell if it was a shadow or a blur that would zoom pass by. She would ignore it and it never bothered her.

However, when her roommates had gone out and she was all alone in the room, Nikki started seeing more sinister appearances. Shadows that remained there for longer, but still disappeared when she turned her gaze towards it. Nikki decided that from now on, she would leave the bathroom light on. At times, she left the bathroom door open to let more light into the room. She did not want to sleep in complete darkness.

One evening after sleeping for a few hours, Nikki was wide awake. No sound had woken her up and she was still alone in the room. Her roommates had not come back yet. As she stared at the ceiling, she could see on her right, a dark figure standing at the bathroom door. Slowly and not wanting to agitate whatever it was, Nikki slowly turned her head towards the right. Her heart was pounding hard and her muscles tensed up. She was ready to fight or run for her life. As she turned slowly, she could see it was a figure of a woman with long dark hair. Although the light in the bathroom was bright, she could not see what 'she' was wearing. She seemed to have a rather dark robe on. Sweat poured from Nikki's face and body, and she decided it was time to see it all. The moment she turned her head completely to look at the figure, it disappeared. Nikki jumped out of bed and switched on all the lights in her room and closed the bathroom door.

She ended up having difficulty falling back to sleep and decided it was best to switch off the lights in her room, leave the bathroom door open and the bathroom light on.

There were other evenings when Nikki was alone in the room and she could see the dark lady apparition by the bathroom door. Every time Nikki turned her head to confirm its presence, the spirit had disappeared. Eventually, Nikki decided to ignore it. At times, Nikki would mockingly challenge it by saying out loud, "You're blocking the light!" Sometimes, the lady spirit disappeared on cue.

The construction company became a lot busier as the construction project made more progress. Her roommates would also be posted at other sites, which meant that they did not come back to their room for a few nights. Nikki was not afraid of being alone. After working under the hot tropical sun, all Nikki wanted to do was take a long shower and then sleep.

One stormy night, Nikki was woken up suddenly. Her door had flung open. It alarmed Nikki, she was worried about an intruder. She jumped out of bed, clutching onto a heavy Maglite-china-clone flashlight and tiptoed towards her room door. She was sure she had locked the door before getting to bed.

She wandered out loud if someone had opened the door. Nikki went down the small hallway and checked the upstairs main door. This door, which had two separate locks, and still very much locked. There was no way in or out except through this door. Nikki went back to her room and locked her room door. She stared at her door, waiting for an intruder to re-open the door but nothing happened. She fell asleep a few hours later.

It was not the only incident. Every time Nikki had slept alone in the room, the door would mysteriously open itself. Nikki would always peek out the main door to check for any intruders but found nothing. For the next 3 weeks, every time Nikki was alone in the room, the same thing would happen.

However, when her roommates were there, nothing happened.

One Saturday evening, Nikki's workmates had brought her out for drinks. By the time she had reached her room, Nikki realised two things. One, she was going to be sleeping alone in the room yet again that night and the other thing was that she realised she was ebriated!

Nikki waltzed around and began to talk slowly and loudly, "Look, I am locking the door! See the door is really locked!"

She jumped onto her bed, tummy first and she saw in the corner of her eye, the dark figure standing by the bathroom door.

Nikki turned on her side and patted on the bed, "Come on, let's talk!"

This time she could see as clearly as she could the shadow was indeed a 'woman' dressed in black with long black hair. Nikki could not see her face clearly, but she could definitely see her dark skin and she had gleaming red eyes.

Nikki had lost her inhibition and was not afraid, and so went on, "Come on! You tell me what you want? I don't disturb you. But you always disturb me. Come on talk to me! I give you my full attention. Tell me what you want."

The lady in black did not utter a single word. She slowly faded as Nikki became drowsy and dozed off.

After that, Nikki did not experience any door opening incidences anymore. From time to time, she still sees the lady in black by the bathroom door. Nikki does feel a sense of relief when she sees her 'presence'. It means she is at least not sleeping alone in the room.

Angel & The Staff-house

Angel was one of Nikki's roommates. Like Nikki, she was also from the Philippines and worked for the same construction company. Angel had issues living away from home, in a foreign country but that all got better once she met Jerome. Jerome was working for a different construction company that was also working on the same mega national construction project in this country. When they first met, she was 24 whilst he was 27. She never imagined how fast their relationship would develop and how comfortable she was with him. She wondered if it was real love or homesickness. Angel kept telling herself not to think too much about the future. She needed him, he needed her for both their emotional and physical needs.

Angel stayed at the staff house at Pintu Malim village. At first, she had not noticed any oddities, other than it was a very old but large house. The renovation and new coat of paint could not hide its true age. Angel did not always sleep in that house as her boyfriend had his own place, which was a company house shared with other men. She spent most nights at her beau's as it was more comfortable, and Jerome did not have to share his room with anyone.

However, one day, Jerome's housemates had a loud

party in the house, and they both decided it was best to sleepover at Angel's house. Conveniently, Angel's other roommates had to work outstation, which meant Angel and Jerome had the room to themselves.

Like delinquent school children, Angel and Jerome snuck to the first floor of the staff-house, laughing and giggling. Angel made sure the upstairs main door was locked. The upstairs was eerily quiet, they thought they would have the whole floor to themselves.

"You could scream all night if you want, and no one would hear you," Jerome laughed as he pecked sensually on Angel's neck. She pulled him to their room, and after locking the room, they both peeled off their clothes so fast that it should have been made an Olympic sport. They jumped into bed with vigor and turned their past experiences into raucous new climatic highs.

After it was over, the couple in their post-coital perspiration talked about the things they missed about in the Philippines and their hopes and dreams. One thing about Jerome was that he was a loud person. He didn't just talk loudly, he also always laughed loudly. Angel adored this about him, he reminded her of the bustling life that she once knew.

Out of the blue, Jerome start shivering, "This room has gotten cold suddenly."

"It's the sweating that is overcooling you, Jerome," Angel concluded. She did not feel cold at all. Angel picked up his shirt and briefs from the floor and flung it to him, "You should sleep with some clothes on otherwise it will get too cold for you."

Angel switched off the light and slept next to Jerome. Angel had a vivid dream where she was confronted by a woman who was possibly her age, but whose face she could not see well. She could not really hear what the woman was saying so she came closer and closer to her. Angel was also hoping she could properly see the woman's face. She got so close to her face; she could feel her cold breath on to her face. Suddenly, the woman let out a bone-chilling scream and this woke Angel up.

Everything was dark, and slowly Angel could make out the dark silhouette of the furniture. This was her room, the room she was supposed to sleep in every night. She felt safe again. She was thankful it was just a dream. Yet, she wondered what the dream was all about.

It was at this moment Angel heard an eerie sound, which was coming from inside the room. She grabbed her mobile phone and turned on the flashlight mode of the phone. Slowly, Angel moved the flashlight from one end of the room to another.

"Who's there?" Angel was sure someone was there in the room. She prayed and hoped no one would answer her.

The sound grew louder and louder and she realised the sound was coming from next to her. It was Jerome. There was something wrong with him. His eyes were wide open, and his face looked strained. Even though she had shone the light on to him, Jerome did not turn his head towards her. His arms and hands were stretched out flat on the bed, and his fingers were clawing into the mattress.

"Jerome, wake up!" It was then she noticed how tense his neck was and his chest was barely moving. Jerome was choking. Angel pounded on his chest to wake him up, but to no avail. Crying in panic, she shook Jerome to wake him up. Was he really asleep? His eyes are wide open. Angel let out a prayer to God, to ask for mercy and mercy was granted.

Jerome jumped out of bed, clutching his neck. His eyes were bewildered, gasping for breath; he frantically scrambled to get his pants from the floor.

"We have to get out of here."

"Jerome, calm down. I think you had sleep paralysis. It's okay. I had that once before."

"No, no. A bad woman was strangling me. GET OUT ANGEL! It's not safe!"

There was no time to explain. Angel put on her clothes

as quickly as how it had come off in the first place and they dashed out of the bedroom and into the main hallway. Jerome grabbed Angel's hand and ran towards the main door. They unlocked the door, but they could not pull the door open. As much as Jerome tried to pull it open, the heavy door would not budge. Jerome felt the door handle become colder and colder as the hallway lights flickered several times. Each flicker lasting longer than the other.

"Please don't hurt us," Angel started sobbing and praying in between sobs.

Suddenly, the lights had gone out. The hallway was completely dark and quiet. It was so quiet they could both hear their hearts pounding out of their ribcages. Jerome held Angel tightly and leaned hard against the door. At least he did not have to worry about being attacked from the back. Angel tried to quieten down her sobs. She could see there was something up ahead at the end of the corridor, a shadow moving in the darkness. She veered her eyes away for fear of provoking what it was that stood there in the pitch black.

A loud banging startled the couple. It was from behind the door.

"Open up! Is everyone alright? "

Angel felt a sense of relief it was a familiar voice. It was one of their co-workers living downstairs.

"Please help. We can't open the door." Angel pleaded.

Instinctively, Jerome turned and pulled the door handle and the door opened with ease. The couple was greeted by intrusive flashlights, which brought much relief after their ordeal.

"The door seems to be working, but the lights are not. Must be a tripped fuse. Anyone turned on any hairdryers or something?"

The house fuse-box was reset, and the lights came back on.

The other tenants noticed how ruffled Angel and Jerome were and tried to reassure them, "It's an old house, the electrical wiring isn't going to be great, but it is still safe."

They had no idea what the couple had experienced. Angel and Jerome decided not to disclose anything. Deciding it was not worth the risk, they drove back to Jerome's place.

The next day, Jerome shared the full encounter with Angel. He was sleeping soundly when he was awoken by a womanly figure who was sitting on his chest and was strangling him. He could see her dark arms and felt her cold unearthly hands over his neck. He could barely breathe and tried his best to fight her, but she was so strong. She was screaming at Jerome to never ever be in the room. He thought he was going to die. There were several deep blue and dark red bruises around Jerome's neck. He had to wear his collar up at work so that no one could see them.

Angel never came back to the room. She requested for different accommodation arrangements.

One day, Angel met Nikki and she decided to share her frightening experience with her. After telling her everything, Angel was puzzled why Nikki did not seem shocked by the whole revelation. Nikki explained she knew about the other 'woman' in the room. Nikki wondered what Jerome did to upset the spirit. To this day, Nikki could only conclude that it must have been Jerome's brashness and loudness. Perhaps.

Maria & The Staff-house

Maria was one of Nikki's roommates after Angel had moved out officially. Maria is also a Filipino but unlike Nikki, she is distinctly from Mindanao, which is commonly known as Southern Philippines. Maria was what others would call a more conservative Filipino.

The first day Maria moved in, Nikki could see how uneasy she was with the room. Maria was not comfortable. Maria wondered if this was due to homesickness. This was the first year of working abroad and she had already missed her family, especially her mother.

She had asked Nikki if anything had happened in the area. Nikki was at first puzzled by the vague questions but decided to reassure Maria that everything was safe in this area.

From the first night, Maria would insist that they left a small night light on, and Maria prayed each night before going to bed. The other roommates tried their best to be understanding and accommodated to her request.

By habit, Maria was always checking every corner of the room before sleeping, and her roommates did their best not to notice Maria's peculiar behaviour. Eventually,

Maria checked the room less often before going to bed, and slowly settled down.

Who could not fall in love with this old large house? Maria would wake up to the majestic view of the serene tea-coloured river and their backyard was abundant with mature and productive rambutan fruit trees. Monkeys from the surrounding jungle would swing by every two to three days in full troupe to feast on the rambutans and other fruits that grew here. Maria, whose family were farmers, started growing papayas and chili plants with ease as the soil was very fertile.

One Thursday evening, Maria was alone in the room. Her roommates were working in a different district and were sleeping elsewhere for the night. Feeling lonely and missing home, she decided to video-call her mother using her mobile phone. She was very happy to see her face and smiled as tears streamed down her face as they both professed how much they had missed each other. Her mother talked about the latest happenings at home, which was really gossip, the people who were dating each other or gotten engaged, whilst Maria shared with her about the people she had met.

Out of the blue, Maria noticed her mother's face had changed. She looked worried. Before she could ask her mother, her mother asked Maria, "I thought you're on your own tonight. Who is that woman standing behind you?"

Maria should have known better, but she spun around and saw the bathroom door was opened behind her. There was no one there, and yet all the hairs on her arms stood up and her body shivered in fear.

"There's no one here, Ma," Maria whispered.

"She's still there, Maria. Get out of the room now!" Her mother was almost screaming and got disconnected immediately.

Maria did not hesitate. She sprinted out of the room and made up her mind to head downstairs so as to be in the company of the male occupants of the house. As she turned right towards the main door of the upstairs hallway, she bumped into someone.

It was a child, a young girl who was probably around 7 years old. Maria asked herself, "Whose child is this?" The young girl whose long hair covered most of her face giggled and ran down the corridor, in the direction away from the main door. Maria was unsure of what to do. The child stopped by one of the doors and the door had mysteriously opened. The girl gestured for Maria to follow her. Maria; without thinking, started walking towards the girl and the door that had mysteriously opened up. She did not remember that particular room having existed in the first place. Everything inside her was telling her not to go, and yet she could not stop her body walking towards imminent danger.

Her mobile phone suddenly rang and that somehow broke whatever was binding Maria's body. Maria spun around and dashed towards the main door, jumping down a flight of stairs and onto the ground floor, startling the male housemates who were relaxing in the living room lobby.

When she had calmed down, she called back her mother who had been trying her best to reach her but no one was answering.

Worried, Maria's mother had contacted a relative whose aunt was living in the same country as Maria. This 'aunt' was a spiritual 'mediator' or exorcist, depending on how the situation was. She visited Maria's room and performed a spiritual mediation service. Maria did not understand what was happening. She merely sat patiently in one corner of the room and watched this aunt seemingly talking to the thin air.

After a long while, the aunt stood up and called Maria, "It's done, the spirit only wanted to play. She did not want to harm you. I made her promise not to disturb you again." The aunt patted Maria's hand reassuringly. However, Maria refused to be in the room alone. She would only sleep in the room when the other roommates were there, and they had to leave a night light on.

One day, Maria told Nikki what had happened. Maria noticed how Nikki seemed unfazed by the story.

"You know about this woman ghost already?"

Nikki nodded without saying a single word.

It wasn't the last time Maria had a supernatural encounter.

One day, Maria was not well. She had caught a bad flu and at the same time she was having a rather heavy menstrual bleeding. She could not go to work and took the day off. Laying down in bed, she slept for most of the morning. In the afternoon, she had to go to the bathroom. She could barely walk as she was feeling very dizzy. The bathroom floor itself was wet and slippery and somehow Maria had slipped, fallen down onto the tiled floor and lost consciousness.

"Maria. Maria, you have to get up." Maria opened her eyes, the light in the bathroom was blinding but she could see the silhouette of a young woman who was pulling her up to her feet.

"Maria, you have to get better. Change your clothes and go and rest on the bed."

Maria got some new clothes and changed and then the woman helped Maria to her bed and tucked her in. Even though she could see everything else in the room clearly by now, the face of the woman seemed unclear and blurry.

Maria knew who she was and even though she was not well and seemingly vulnerable, Maria was not scared. She watched the spirit walking back towards the bathroom and disappeared. Whatever she was, she was now watching over and protecting Maria. Before she fell asleep, Maria thanked aloud the spirit.

The Pretty

Farah was a nursing student whom had shared a story about the time she had a clinical work attachment at the hospital in the Capital. She had read Real Ghost stories of Borneo 1 and was shocked to read one of the stories as she had a connected event.

She was already in her 2nd year of nursing college. Student nurses must undertake clinical attachments to gain work experience in the hospitals as well as clinics. There was pride and joy to be dressed in their student nurse uniforms, observing and sometimes helping their nurse compatriots. However, it was not all fine and dandy. It was not about the fact that Farah was in the presence of her sick and unwell patients, it was the other things she could see that are invisible to most.

Sometimes she could see apparitions, some appeared as tall shadow-like figures whilst others appeared as womanly figures whose long hair never revealed their faces. They would appear standing and motionless near one or two of the patients in the hospital wards. Farah would feel apprehensive and yet, she did her best to ignore them.

"If I pretend I did not see you, then I hope you will pretend you did not notice that I can see you."

Her father, who was aware of her 'gift', kept on reminding Farah to ignore them. Her father advised her to recite a prayer before entering the hospital. She should not stare, look or interact with whatever she saw.

"They are busy with their own doings, as we, humans are busy in with our own lives," her father had told her.

One day, she was told her colleagues and her would be visiting the Intensive Care Unit (ICU) wards, where they would have a chance to experience and work aside hard-working, dedicated critical-care nurses who were treating and tending to patients on life-support machines. Her colleagues and her were to be there for two days.

The excitement quickly died down the moment Farah entered the ICU ward. She saw tall faceless shadow-like figures with long dark slender limbs. Some were hovering around the patients and their beds. It was her first day in an intense clinical environment, with many alarms and beeps going off, and the sound of life support machines including lung ventilators continuously working without fail. To top everything, she could see the demon-like supernatural beings there. She was not happy; this was very difficult for her. Her nurse mentor there, Sister Midah, sensed Farah was troubled by something beyond the sight of the critically unwell. However, Farah did not share what she could see. She didn't want to look silly or even assumed not sane.

Sister Midah brought her to help her tend to a very ill 30-plus-year-old patient who was fighting for her life. The medically-induced-coma made her look like she was in a deep sleep. Yet, the patient was connected to an artificial ventilator, which was breathing for her through a tube hose that went straight into her throat and larynx. She had several intravenous tubes going into her body, pumping death-defying drugs. Farah saw a giant faceless shadow-like creature standing over her. It was an unavoidable circumstance. She did her best not to look at the overwhelming creature whilst the both of them tended to the patient's basic needs i.e. cleaning her soiled nappy and then recording her vital physiological stats.

Even though the very unwell lady was in an induced coma and not responsive, she had a very beautiful face. As Farah stared at her, she admired her doll-like face and flawless skin. She seemed so serene even though she was losing the fight against a progressive auto-immune disease, which had led to several of her major organs to fail.

It was at this moment, Farah heard a resonating voice calling out to her, "Pretty. Very Pretty."

Without thinking, she looked up immediately and noticed it was the faceless death-like creature talking to her. As she was staring at it, shapes began to appear from the dark empty face of the creature. Slowly, an image of a human face emerged. It was the doll-like face of her unwell lady patient, eyes still shut.

"Pretty, Very Pretty," it said without moving her lips.

Farah shuddered, and nearly collapsed onto the floor. She stumbled and then ran out of the ICU ward, leaving Sister Midah baffled. Farah had to go home; it was not safe for her to be in the hospital. She briskly headed to her car, she was very uneasy and paranoid that whatever it was, would follow her and hurt her. Farah sensed a dozen shadow-like figures were tailing her. She jumped into her car and drove home fast, not caring for the traffic.

When she got home, she weepily told her father about her ordeal.

"The dark creatures are everywhere; this is as much their world as it is ours. They will not bother us unless we bother them first," he tried to reassure her, but assured she was not. Never in her life had any of 'them' talked to her. The two of them recited prayers and her father advised her to sleep it off. It was still late afternoon, but there was no point in staying awake and worrying. At least that was her father's reasoning.

As Farah laid in her bed, still shaken, she tried to reflect upon the incident. It had only been her first day. She would have to explain to the nurses in the ICU ward what had happened. They would probably ridicule her, she thought. In addition to that, she had one more day to survive.

Farah resolved she could not go back there. She would take a 'Sick Leave' and she would figure out a way in explaining her absence.

"Pretty, isn't she?" A voice echoed in her room. Overhanging over her bed, Farah saw; to her horror, the same giant shadow-like creature, now with the pretty doll-face. Its long-overstretched arms held on to each side of her bed. She could not escape. Frozen in terror, she watched as her patient's face on the creature disappeared, turning it back to a faceless dark creature. Darkness swirled and patterns appeared where the face had been, and then a new face began to form.

Farah screamed so hard that her father ran and broke down her bedroom door. Her father, who himself could see the supernatural, saw the apparition hovering over his daughter's bed. He tried to punch it as he grabbed and pulled away his daughter to safety.

"My face, it has got my face now!" Farah was hysterical, trying to escape her own father's embrace. She shook violently in fear, as her mother and siblings did their best to calm her down. Her father called his brother, a traditional healer and an expert in matters relating to supernatural disturbances. Luckily, he lived next door and was there almost immediately.

When her uncle arrived, he saw the dark demon with its long slender limbs was still in Farah's bedroom, and to his shock, it had what appeared to be a facsimile of Farah's face, eyes closed and expressionless.

Her uncle called up his friends and together with Farah's father, they sat in her room, forming an incomplete circle around the creature. They started with loud reciting of Holy mantras, followed by reading of Holy Verses. Farah's father could not help himself from crying openly as he recited in desperation to keep this ghoul from his daughter. Meanwhile, Farah, who was still in shock, was kept in a separate room, with her mother and all the relatives there doing their best to soothe her. Farah was asked to recite prayers too.

According to her father, Farah's image slowly disappeared from the creature, and it reverted to its faceless form. After many hours of reciting Holy Verses and reciting mantra, her uncle told the demon to leave Farah alone. When it finally agreed to the family's demand, the demon itself disappeared into thin air.

Farah took the week off and stayed at home. She was never left alone during that time. Her family hosted daily prayer functions with the rest of the extended family. The official excuse was that Farah was overwhelmed with work-study stress and family issues. Farah continued to see and sense the paranormal beings and more. However, they never bothered her and had never followed her home.

Much later on, Farah heard that the lady patient who she tended to, had actually died the same afternoon she ran away.

The Recording

Two people introduced me to Tina's recording. It was a short 10 second audio clip. I was not sure what to make of it. This is her story.

In Kota Kinabalu city, Tina, an unemployed school dropout, initially didn't mind the stagnant life. Like other girls, she tried to find work, but she never got any interviews or offers for the jobs she wanted. On the other hand, the other jobs that were available were too lowly paid.

That was the dilemma, so Tina felt it was better to be unemployed, whilst the great opportunity awaited her. She would stay at home as her friends seemed to have their own lives either in full time employment, in their busy married lives or in further studies. As much as she wanted to simply watch TV, or chat and play with her mobile phone all day long, being at home came at a price. She was always inundated with all these menial tasks such as taking care of the children i.e. her troublesome toddler nephews and nieces, and cooking.

Luckily, Tina decided not to renew her driving licence. She made up some excuse that she had a traumatising 'near accident' and she could not drive the car anymore.

She knew if she did not do this, she would end up being the permanent family chauffeur - stuck in perpetual school runs.

Even so, the house had become a free day-care centre for her siblings' children, which she found very annoying. It was another unpaid job and yet she believed it carried all the 'employers' expectations of proper employment. Of course, there was no benefits let alone paid leave for her. It was truly modern-day slavery. Tina never shared with anyone, but she frequently yearned for the 'knight in shining armour' to rescue her from her predicament.

One day, her grandmother, who lived in the same house, had fallen down the stairs. She had a serious hip bone fracture and had to be admitted for major hip surgery. It was going to be a big surgery and she was expected to be in hospital for some time. The common practice was that a family member should be there at the hospital, to help her grandmother with daily things and to keep the rest of the family updated with any progress or otherwise. Her parents, uncles and aunts agreed that the only unemployed adult was to be assigned to this task. Tina didn't have any say in this. In her household, the unemployed are not allowed to vote or participate in family discussions.

Tina loved her grandmother when she was younger. Now that her senile grandmother was different i.e. she talked much less and grumbled more, Tina felt disconnected from her grandmother. Nevertheless, Tina did her best to appear obliging to the role of caretaker.

The good news was that the orthopedic surgeons deemed the hip surgery a success, which meant they didn't kill her on the operating table. However, her grandmother had to stay in the hospital ward until her pain had subsided and she had some degree of mobility.

Most of the time, Tina's grandmother was always asleep. Sometimes she was asleep peacefully - thanks to the painkillers she had been prescribed, whilst other times she was grimacing in pain. She would wake up to eat and then be checked on and cleaned up by the nurses and the physiotherapist.

Tina didn't have to do anything really. She would sit next to her grandmother's hospital bed, strapped her wireless headphones to her ears and played with her mobile phone all day and all-night long. She would watch online videos and chatted with some of her male admirers cum stalkers, who had no idea of the person behind her fake Instagram and Snapchat accounts. There was nothing else for her to do in the hospital. This was all acceptable and fine for Tina, until her phone ran out of credit. Unfortunately for her, there was no Wi-Fi or free internet. Now she was dying of boredom. When her parents, aunts and uncles came around during the evenings, Tina asked for money to buy phone credits, and even when she complained loudly, they didn't oblige.

Now, she was really dying of boredom. She occasionally

talked to the nurses and staff in the ward. They seemed busy though she was able to have the random conversations with them. She thought about hanging out with the hospital security guards, but their minds can be so single-tracked.

It was at this time that she began to notice Mimah, a middle-aged Malay lady whose bed was next to her grandmother's. Mimah was walking about here and there, she did not seem to belong in the ward. She had been talking to herself frequently. It spooked Tina initially. When she asked the staff about Mimah, she was told that she had been there for several years! She had been awaiting to be discharged from the hospital but none of her extended family members were willing to take responsibility for her, in view of her mental health illness and other unknown family issues.

Hence, she was stuck in hospital, waiting for the social welfare department to make new living arrangements, but somehow, she got 'lost in the system'. Other than the ward nurses, she had no one else taking care of her. None of her family members bothered to visit her. It was a sad plight.

At first, Tina felt apprehensive and did her best to avoid Mimah, especially when Mimah seemed to be having these long conversations with herself. She was clearly as mad as a hatter. It was a big contrast between the very talkative Mimah and her quiet sleeping grandmother.

In the middle of the night, the ward was usually quiet. It would be dark as all the lights were switched off, except the ones in the main corridor and the nurses' station. Resting in the comfy armchair next to her grandmother's bed, Tina could not fall asleep, she had been thinking about what she should do with her life. She could not piece anything together as she became distracted by her neighbour. Mimah seemed to be having a debate with herself. Tina peeked through the separating curtains to peek into Mimah's side. Mimah was talking to herself again, her hands swaying ungracefully in front of her.

Bored and without any internet connection, Tina amused herself with a new idea. She used her mobile phone to make a short audio recording of Mimah. She would have preferred to capture a video, but it was too dark. She thought it would be funny. She would share it with her friends - if they ever meet up - or better still, use it to scare her nephews and nieces. If only she had credit in her mobile phone. Tina started laughing to herself at the thought. It was at this moment, Tina felt quite cold and the air around her grew heavy. She wondered if it was the central air-conditioning that had finally kicked in. She quickly drifted to a deep slumber.

Tina did not sleep peacefully; she dreamt she was with Mimah in a dried-out and rotting fruit orchard. Mimah held on to Tina as she warned her not to let them catch her. She pointed to a burning wooden stilted house, which had appeared out of nowhere. Out of this house, three men appeared; flames were engulfing their bodies, and yet their heads seemed intact. To Tina's horror, the men's faces were blank empty, with zero facial features. They began to run towards Tina and although they had no mouths, she could hear them shout at her as they chased after Tina and Mimah.

When Tina finally woke up sweating and almost screaming from her nightmare, she found herself sleeping on a bench outside the ward. Passersby would stare and passed judgement before ignoring her and going on with their business. Tina wondered how she ended up on the bench and concluded she must have sleepwalked somehow. She shrugged it off and headed back to the ward and her grandmother's bed. She was going to take a shower, and as she prepared her toiletries, she noticed her mobile phone was by her grandmother's ward side table. Tina grabbed it quickly. She thought about how lucky she was that no one had stolen it. It was then she remembered the audio recording. As she played the audio recording, one of the nurses came up to her and asked what she was up to. Before she could answer, they both realised that it was Mimah's voice and there was another voice caught in the recording. It was a man's voice; it was not clear what he was saying.

"Who was Mimah talking to?" The nurse asked suspiciously.

"She was talking on her own, I don't know whose voice that is. She was all alone last night." Tina was baffled.

"What! You should not be recording her. That's not right. Are you trying to make fun of her?" The nurse was clearly upset, but she seemed more spooked by what she had heard.

After showering, Tina wondered whose voice it was. She kept playing the audio over and over again. The voice sounded so familiar and yet it wasn't. The short audio spooked her every time she played it. She had hoped that the more she played it, the more she would get used to the feeling, and the goosebumps should eventually disappear. However, it only seemed to intensify.

Rumours about Tina's recording and the unknown male voice in the audio spread like wildfire amongst the ward nurses. Some of the nurses would come up to Tina to listen to the 'man's voice' and would get quite upset about it. They did not even feel comfortable to go in pairs for their toilet breaks. They had to go in trios! It caused quite a bit of a scare amongst the staff. The ward manager decided to contact Tina's family and advised them to bring Tina back home as she was deemed a nuisance and disruptive. Tina protested, saying that Mimah was actually the one who was disruptive, going on talking to herself every single time. Everyone in Tina's family took turns scolding Tina for her disrespectful and immature behaviour. They also scolded her for being useless and unemployed.

142

Tina found herself at home, fuming in anger. She could not believe how ungrateful her family had been for the work she had done for them. She was caught in a storm of her own disappointments. She locked herself in her room and thought about leaving home for good, perhaps hitch a ride from a friend or even a stranger and leave town to anywhere. She was shouting to herself, and in all the heat of her anger, she slapped her own face a few times. Feeling numb from the rage and pain, she sobbed uncontrollably.

And then a familiar voice came around. It was a man's voice. It was the same male voice. She looked up and in front of her appeared a dark silhouette sitting in front of her. It had rather long arms, a thin body and a featureless face. She tried to run away but found herself frozen in terror. She wanted to scream yet no sound came from her mouth. She could hardly breathe as her own chest tightened so much; she could feel her ribs about to snap. The apparition changed appearance and looked more like the burning figures that was chasing her in her dreams, except this time, the entity was not engulfed in flames. It was repeating the same thing over and over, each time becoming slightly ever clearer, until the moment she heard it all in complete clarity in her head. Everything around her turned to black and Tina lost consciousness.

Her uncle had broken down her bedroom door the next morning. Her family was very worried when she didn't open the door, no matter how many times Tina's mother tried to call her out. The following week, Tina remained quiet and kept mostly to herself.

Eventually, she called up a good friend of hers and told her everything that had happened. Tina was tired of everything; she wanted to live, to have a life that was hers. Against her family's advice, she moved out to live with her friend and got a below-minimum-wage job as a waitress in a small 'kopitiam' restaurant. She still visited her family during the weekends, driving in her own small car that she bought using her earnings. Tina never shared what was actually revealed by the apparition. The whole incident changed her life, she began to live and owned her life.

On the other hand, Mimah was still pleasantly in the ward, waiting for social welfare department's arrangements. She continues to have frequent conversations with 'herself' up to this day.

Mimi & The Park

I met 'Mimi', a middle-aged mother (she would dread that term) at my clinic. She reminded me that we were school-mates. Even though I was trying to ascertain her teenage daughter's ailment, Mimi and I ended up chatting about quite a few things under the sun. Despite my constant apologies, her daughter was not too pleased with the both of us, as it was supposed to be her time with the doctor and not her mother's!

Mimi ran a small family restaurant at the Sungai Basong Recreational Park, which was in Tutong town. Having worked and lived in Tutong town, I was quite familiar with this restaurant. It was the first time I had ever seen a Malay woman make an Indian roti or martabak (I still don't understand the difference between the two!) The Sungai Basong park was a few minutes' walk away from the hospital and the clinic that I had previously worked at. After work, I would usually either walk or cycle around the area. There was a large man-made pool there as well as a few smaller ponds. There were also a few cultural installations: small stilted huts with cultural displays, representing the five ethnic groups of Tutong district.

She shared a few stories with me with regards to the incidents that she had witnessed or have heard of the park.

Mimi's family's restaurant was situated inside a small bungalow hut, next to one of the smaller ponds. One day, Mimi had been tasked to prepare several dishes for the Tutong town celebrations. She had undertaken a contract to cater for a few hundred people during the town council function. Hence, the day before, Mimi, her mother and their main chef of 18 years, Hamid, had slaved away from noon till late night at the restaurant whilst her cousin; Jan, loitered and smoked the night away outside. He was like their security guard for the night.

They had been busy preparing their famous 'Ungkil', a chili paste delicacy or 'sambal' which was enhanced with 'Ikan Bakulan'. 'Ikan Bakulan' is a smaller Tuna fish species (Thunnus tonggol species, to be precise). The preparations were painstakingly arduous, especially with the volume and the consistency that was needed. They were finishing off the last batch when the otherwise silent night in the park was interrupted by a heart-stopping sound of the clanging of metal in the area. The sound was followed by another sound, which sounded like a heavy piece of metal being dragged on an asphalt road.

"Who would be here in the park at this time of the night?" Mimi was trying to calm her chef, Hamid. Hamid was particularly nervous about working late night. He had seen enough 'things' at the park.

The sound went on; something hitting a large piece of metal bar, perhaps. The sound rung eerily all over. Mimi instructed Jan to find out what it was. Jan looked around; his eyes focused on the orange sodium light highway which was adjacent to the park. The highway was void of cars and activity. Jan had a bad feeling as he felt goosebumps all over. Reluctantly, he took his flashlight and shone it around the dark park. The pavement lights there had been switched off to discourage the public from loitering at the park at night. The only lights came from the fluorescent lights of the restaurant. The sound went on continuously.

Jan had to stop the sound, otherwise Mimi was going to make him investigate the source. Jan did not want to meet the 'source' of the sound.

"Who is that? Stop what you are doing!"

Initially there was no response - and then there were three heart-rattling loud bangs, like a pile of steel girders being dropped onto the road. At least that was what Jan thought. He had worked for a construction company before quitting for a sedentary lifestyle i.e. stay at home and remain unemployed.

Then the dragging sound came again. He lit his cigarette whilst he pondered what he should do next. There was no way he was going to walk around the park on his own.

"Jan, go check it out now!" Mimi insisted, "bring Hamid with you!"

Hamid was not taking any chances, so he grabbed his 'parang' or machete. He had seen enough apparitions and as annoying as it was to him, he was more scared of robbers and thieves lurking in the dark.

Leaving Mimi and her mother all alone in the restaurant, Hamid could see the mother and daughter arguing on whether or not to pack the batches of Ungkil into large containers and bring it home. Hamid didn't like the idea of leaving them behind but he had to obey their instructions.

Mimi and her mother eventually stuck to their original plan, which was to leave it there in the restaurant as the main access road would be cordoned off by police the next day for the town wide celebrations. As they waited for the men to make their rounds, they heard a faint rustling sound near the hut. Alarmed, they peeked out of the kitchen window. They both noticed a sinister-looking figure darting in the darkness around the restaurant hut. It looked like a thin person running between the trees and towards the edge of the small pond. They could not make out what it was wearing. Its silhouette looked less and less humanoid the longer they stared at it. Undaunted, Mimi's elderly mother grabbed a large kitchen knife whilst Mimi herself grabbed a sturdy and trusted meat cleaver. If it was coming into the kitchen, the mother and daughter team was going to take it down!

They waited in anticipation for a confrontation of their lives.

Meanwhile, Jan and Hamid went around the pitch-black park with Jan's flashlight being the only source of light. Jan used his flashlight to screen the area in front of him and beyond, in a random and wide pattern. Jan hated surprises, especially of the unnatural kind. The metallic sound was continuous and no matter what they said, it continued to echo around them. When they reached one end of the park, which was near the 'stilted display huts', the sound had changed its direction, as though acting as a beacon... of horror. This time it was coming from the cultural display huts. The huts were on their right and the jungle and the trail leading up to the hills, were in front of them.

"It's not worth it," Jan whispered to Hamid.

"What is not worth it?" Hamid replied.

"I think we better go back. It's not worth it."

Hamid nodded in agreement, both men were terrified of being there. They felt an overwhelming hellraising 'presence' surrounding the area.

They turned back and slowly headed towards the restaurant hut. The restaurant was the only structure in the park that had white fluorescent lights. Its light emanating like a beacon of hope in the starless night.

Jan, at first thought Hamid was shuffling his feet, whilst Hamid thought it was Jan who was doing so. Instinctually, they looked at each other and immediately realised an oddity. There was an ominous feeling that they were being followed. It was when they realised that every step they both made, there were unaccounted footstep sounds. It was no echo. Hamid was about to look behind him, when Jan, without warning, yelled out some obscenities and sprinted away. Hamid had no choice but to run after Jan.

Hamid felt a heavy pressure sensation on both his shoulders as though something was piggybacking on him. His body could not run fast as his legs grew heavy. Without stopping and looking behind, he unsheathed his 'parang' and slashed blindly the thin air behind his back, whilst muttering Holy Verses. The sensation disappeared, his legs felt more normal and he ran even faster, catching up to Jan.

By the time Jan and Hamid reached the restaurant, they crashed into the plastic chairs outside the restaurant, startling Mimi and her mother into screams of terror.

Eventually, everyone calmed down and after reciting prayer verses, the four of them sat in the restaurant waiting for daylight. They ignored the continuous metallic sound which eventually disappeared on its own.

By dawn, the world of the living had reclaimed the restaurant, and everyone did their part to deliver the delicacies.

***

Personally, I have never gone up close to see what is inside the huts. I have always had a feeling that I should stay away. Even when cycling there, I would never venture beyond the jungle trail entrance, especially when dusk time. I could not explain the feeling at that time.

Dr. Aammton Alias

Sleeping Beside A Window

Original story from Nur <u>Khayrin</u> Sofiya Noorismawarddy, from PAP Hjh Masna high school (Year 8)

I could barely keep my eyes open, as the car poorly negotiated the narrow bumpy road to my grandmother's house. There were no streetlights and the car's headlights could barely illuminate the road on this particularly dark night. My mother was fast asleep and snoring gracefully in the passenger seat in front, whilst my father was tensely silent. His eyes were wide open and completely focused on driving. I could tell he was not happy about driving these roads, he had to be ready for any horrible surprises. I felt obliged to stay awake, to watch over him, in case he too fell asleep, but in the end, I caved in and dozed off. When the car slowed down and came to an abrupt halt, my father's deep voice woke us up, "We're here."

My grandmother's house was a wooden stilted house, with grey weathered wooden stairs in the front and a red vernacular roof. Unlike our house, grandmother's house was still using the old and energy inefficient incandescent lightbulbs, which barely lit the outside of the house, and yet gave a romantic vintage look. A dim yellow light behind the white curtains of the living room meant grandmother was inside. She was always at home, as she had no other place to go.

My parents got out of the car and we brought out our 'weekend-stay' luggage. When we climbed up the short flight of wooden stairs, each step creaked so loudly it would have woken up the neighbours, but my grandmother had no neighbours.

She should have heard us by then but she was hard of hearing. My mother had to knock hard on the door and shout out for my grandmother several times before she finally opened the door. My grandmother stood in the doorway, her 'sarong' wrapped around her waist, her white hair tied back in a bun and her face had deep wrinkles.

My mother dropped her luggage and embraced my grandmother tightly.

"It has been a long time," said my grandmother over my mother's shoulder, her voice hoarse. Her hollow eyes drifted, and when her eyes focused on me, they widened.

"Oh my…," my grandmother took a deep breath, pulling away from my mother, who was about to speak.

I stiffened as my grandmother walked on trembling and seemingly unsteady towards me. She pinched my chin with her thumb and index finger. I did not dare to breathe as she gazed deep into my eyes as though she was searching for my soul. Uncountable minutes passed, and she finally let go.

She turned towards my mother. "She has her grandfather's eyes," she whispered, grinning toothlessly.

My father was not too happy to see her, and he could not help himself from frowning. He has never been fond of my grandmother. Ever since I was young, he would prevent my mother from taking me to visit my grandmother. They would argue but, in the end, my father would always win the argument. However, this time, the tables have turned.

"So why did you call us to stay with you?" my father asked in a rather sharp tone. My mother gestured with her eyes to him. It was a stern warning not to start what she will make sure he cannot finish. My grandmother pretended not to notice, she only looked at me, gathering her thoughts and when she thought she was ready, she turned to my mother.

"Ever since your… your father's death…," she whispered, and paused for a long time to maintain her composure, "Strange things have been happening lately. They frighten me. I need some company." My grandfather had passed away three months ago. We were told that he had died of a heart attack and that several relatives had seen some rather strange rashes all over his body.

My mom's face looked ashen, "What strange things?"

154

For a moment, my grandmother did not reply. Instead, she stared at one of the windows, her eyes this time dull and almost lifeless, "Maybe you'll see."

"Come on," my father suddenly interrupted. He didn't like dramatics, and he was not too pleased at entertaining his mother-in-law. Impatiently, he nudged me through the door, and we headed towards the guest bedroom. I looked back and saw my mother and grandmother were busy chatting.

As I entered the guest bedroom, I was happy to see the queen-sized bed against the wall next to a window. I was tired and yet overjoyed to finally be able to sleep on a newly-made bed. I literally jumped on the bed.

"I know you're tired," my father acknowledged whilst he placed our luggage near the door. "Just go to sleep. Your mother and I will join you later." I buried my face into the mattress and let out a muffled 'okay.'

Then I heard a click, and the lights went off, followed by the soft sound of a door being gently closed. I shut my eyes and laid down on my side. Oddly enough, the room was cold even though there was only a ceiling fan and no air-conditioner.

Without warning, I felt a spine-chilling uneasiness. There was a low crackle of thunder, followed by the pattering of tiny raindrops. The window to my left had no curtains and I could not help myself from looking through it. Flashes of lightning ripped through the night sky and then the tropical monsoon downpour began.

Annoyed that I definitely would not be able to sleep thanks to the storm, I sat up and watched the lightning and rain 'show' through the window. Lightning struck again but this time a thunderous boom followed it. The lightning struck again and then I saw it. A silhouette by the window.

I froze in terror, wishing it was just a figment of my imagination. Again, a flash of lightning much brighter than before, I could see it so clearly that I could not deny my precarious situation. A silhouette of a woman standing by the windowsill. I choked on my breath. There were no more lightning flashes, but she remained. The woman had chin-length hair, and that she was wearing a traditional outfit called the 'kebaya'.

I closed my eyes in the hopes she would disappear the moment I open my eyes again. I could hear my heart pounding madly, whilst I struggled to control my rapid shallow breathing. I waited for what seemed like an eternity and then opened my eyes.

To my horror, she was still standing there, her hair covered most of her facial features, except for her blood-lustful grin. I thought of running out of the room, but fear overwhelmed my body and I could not move. As I stared at her, she stood there menacingly.

A heaviness overwhelmed me, and I slowly laid back and covered my head with the pillow. I did not realise I had fallen asleep until the next morning when I woke up to find myself alone in the room.

I rubbed my eyes and glanced at the window. There was no trace of the mysterious woman. I was pretty sure she was a ghost.

Relieved, I jumped out of bed. As I was about to leave the room, the back of my neck began to itch. The itch was very troublesome. I actually stopped mid-way towards the door to give it a good damn-right scratch. Then I felt my left arm started to itch too. I rolled up my sleeves, but somehow my eyes strayed towards the window. Then, I began to have a burning sensation where I had scratched. I cried as the pain was overwhelming.

When I looked down at my arm, I could see angry red rings on my skin and pus oozing out. I remembered my grandfather and how he died. I wondered if this was what happened to him. Was I going to die of a 'heart attack' at such a young age? I was barely a teenager. I should not die here.

I dashed out of the bedroom. I had to find my parents and my grandmother. I searched through each room including the living room; I called them out but there was not a single soul in the house.

Crying in desperation, I knew I had to escape from that house. I flung open the main door; and to my relief, I could see the outside luscious green landscape and tall towering trees surrounding the house and garden compound. My diligent father was cutting the overgrown grass, whilst my mother and grandmother were tending to a fruit shrub. I ran towards them and told them about the rash on my arm but when I showed it to them, there was nothing but my smooth forearm. I was glad that I had no malady, it must have been a trick of the mind.

I told them about the woman I had seen last night and that startled my parents. My grandmother stayed quiet. Later that evening, the four of us sat in a prayer circle and prayed for new blessings for the house. My parents slept with me that evening and I slept rather peacefully. We visit my grandmother every weekend. Since then, I had no further 'visitations'.

The Ravine

I had met Fadil at the Mentiri private clinic I worked at. It was good to see him again as he and I had many paintball tournaments together in the United Kingdom. He is currently working on one of the massive tanker ships that carry 'Liquefied Natural Gas' or LNG to and fro Japan. He shared a story with me, which I was initially not keen to write.

It was the year 2012, Fadil, at 27 years old, was up to his usual work arrangement i.e. 4 months out at sea (offshore) and 4 months resting on land (onshore). His wife and his son lived in Sungai Besar village, which is in Kota Batu. Some would refer Kota Batu as the country's 'French Riviera'. There were a number of houses built onto the hillside which faced the slow-moving serene river. There were other houses on the riverbanks too, and many of those houses were wooden stilted houses. They were living with Fadil's in-laws, whose house was on the hilly side of Kota Batu, facing the river. They had a splendid view from there.

His father-in-law; Mr. Maidin, and his brother-in-law; Malik, would hike around the surrounding area. You could say it was a family tradition for father and son to explore their surrounding area, which was covered by pristine jungle, brooks and secret mini-waterfalls. Somehow as soon as Fadil had gotten married, he had also gotten pulled into the male family tradition. Initially, it was hard climbing up the hills, which were slippery at places, but eventually, he became accustomed to it. It became one of the things that he looked forward to once he was onshore again. Fadil hoped that one day he could bring his son to hike around the area.

The area they would trek was vast. Although they had spent many, many weekends exploring the area which extended to Subok village, there was still a lot of unexplored areas for them.

Mr. Maidin had opted to explore a new area which they had previously avoided repeatedly due to frequent rainstorms. It would usually be too slippery to access. They had set off early morning and by the time they reached the new area, it was already noontime. The trees were much taller than the other areas, the air was more humid, and the tree canopy was extensive and let very little sunlight passed through to the ground. At places it was so dark, Fadil had to switch on his headlamp to see the damp ground he was stepping. Brown leaves of various shapes and stages of decomposing littered the ground floor and armies of creepy crawlies scattered away where they had trampled on. This area was sloping downwards, and eventually the vegetation cleared away revealing a seemingly deep gully or ravine. A small clear stream ran through the bottom.

Fadil was the first person to feel very uneasy about exploring the ravine. They did not have safety or proper abseiling equipment. They did have a good strong rope though, but his concerns were beyond equipment. Fadil felt they were unwelcomed in the area. Although there wasn't anyone there, he felt they were being watched by hostile beings.

They tied their rope securely to a large tree trunk and slowly went down the ravine. Without any mishaps, the trio reached the bottom of the rocky ravine and walked towards the sandy stream. The sand was so clean; no sign of human civilization i.e. no litter, and the water was so clear they had a hard time in resisting themselves from drinking it. Untreated and unfiltered water can be very dangerous to drink. Instead, they washed their faces and rested right there on the narrow sandy banks of the shallow stream, admiring how the filtered sunlight danced sparkles on the surface of the stream.

After breaking for a late lunch, they made their way up the rust-brown rock surface of the ravine, doing their best not to slip. Fadil's father-in-law was the first to make it up to the top and he was alarmed. He jumped down on the ground, grabbing on to something. Fadil and Malik who were halfway up could hear a commotion. Fadil climbed even faster, almost letting go off the rope to jump up distances. By the time, he had gotten up to where Mr. Maidin was, he was stumped to see his father-in-law on the ground, gripping tightly for dear life onto the rope. It was no longer tied to the tree!

"Don't just stand there! Help me pull up Malik!" His father-in-law was at the ends of how much he could hold onto the rope.

When Malik finally got up safely, Fadil wanted to scold Malik, but his father-in-law stopped him. One reason not to jump to conclusions was that they had tied the rope together and Mr. Malik being a retired civil engineer, had the habit of double or triple checking on safety such as rope safety. There was no way that rope could have undone itself. There was another matter: if the rope was already secured, then who untied it? Logic dictated that if it was a person with bad intentions, they would have been confronted by the person or persons already. Fadil had his own conclusions but this was neither the place nor the time to discuss such matters.

The dark giant trees looked different this time. Perhaps it was the dimming light that had changed everything; the shadows were longer and they seemed to move aggressively towards them as they picked up the pace to leave the new area. Fadil noticed Malik's eyes scanning wildly on the peripheries of his field of view. Fadil tapped him on his shoulder and then gripped it hard. It was a non-verbal cue, to remind his brother-in-law to ignore whatever was bothering him.

When they left the area and entered more familiar

grounds, his brother-in-law was the first to exclaim his gratefulness for getting out of the situation. Fadil shushed him and told him not to provoke the spirits until they were safely at home. 'Cabul' was the correct term to describe the situation. One should not 'cabul' or jinx the situation.

Fadil had other reasons for being precautious. He could sense that they were being followed. He had wished it was his imagination, but occasionally he saw glimpses of a shadow-like figure silently following, jumping from tree to tree since they left the ravine. When they finally reached the car park, Fadil could see a tall shadow figure, doing its best to blend in with the darkness in between the trees. Fadil told his father what he had seen. His father reassured him and told him to ignore it.

When they got home, Fadil looked around their house, and scanned through the surrounding trees. He had to be sure they had not been followed to their house. Fadil was relieved and was grateful to see his wife and son.

That evening, Fadil was the first to go to his upstairs bedroom, whilst his wife was putting their son to sleep in his own bedroom. Fadil was truly exhausted. Something had caught his eyes. He froze in terror. He could see a clear outline of a tall figure through the thin curtains of his bedroom window. He could not move; he could not shout for help. He could feel his body being pulled towards the window and yet he was not moving at all. He knew it was his soul that was being sucked towards the window. Fadil could see his body behind him as he floated right next to the window. The apparition moved its hand through the window to reach to him and there was nothing he could do to stop it. Just as its demonic hand was about to grab him, it pulled its arm away from him, and Fadil's soul zoomed back into his body. He collapsed onto the floor semi-conscious.

It was later that Fadil found out that his wife had found him staring at the window. No matter how many times she tried to call him, Fadil did not respond. She said a prayer and tapped Fadil's back and after that Fadil fell onto the floor. Since that incident, his wife had always felt that they were being watched, even though she could not see anything suspicious at the window.

She left a few prayer books by the windowsill. Every time they left the room, they would leave the radio on, which was tuned to the Holy Verses channel. With time, neither Fadil nor his wife noticed any oddities outside their bedroom window.

Since the incident, the three men decided to never visit the ravine.

The Adventure Learning

Manisah had just finished her final year exams in nursing college. After this, she would become a full-fledged nurse. The semester had not yet finished. Manisah and her classmates had expected to turn up to the college and somehow skip whatever in-school extracurricular activities and 'chill-ax'. However, the first day after her exams had finished, they were told to attend an 'adventure learning' course in the Temburong district.

She was shocked to learn that they were expected to stay there for 3 nights. Manisah had never camped let alone go to some adventure smack in the middle of 'nowhere'!

You see, the course center is situated in the Temburong district, which is commonly referred to as the green district. Here, the lush tropical rainforest is largely intact and to get there you have to travel by boat or cross the border twice! It was everything it should be: environmentally intact and isolated.

When Manisah told her mother; who was very protective of her eldest petite daughter, her mother nearly had an anxiety attack.

"You can't go there for 4 days! That's 3 whole nights! They don't have electricity at that centre and there is no mobile phone reception! What if you need to call me in the middle of the night?"

Manisah's mother ranted on about her relatives who had encountered unfriendly jungle spirits there. Her mother was unreasonably worried about all the potential mishaps, including the worst and improbable scenario that she would be abducted by one of the 'Bunian' jungle spirits. Her mother tried to persuade her to get a 'medical reason' not to partake in the course.

Of course, Manisah couldn't do that. She didn't want to be labelled by her colleagues as the timid one, it was bad enough that she was the shortest nursing student in her class!

She put on her bravest face and convinced her mother that prayers would protect her from any mishaps, including evil spirits. Manisah's mind was full of doubt and she was scared.

A few days later, after having done a medical fitness examination, she and her twelve classmates started their journey to the Temburong district. Whatever concerns the group had, it disappeared the moment they got onto the coffin-shaped speedboat; the excitement of traversing the river, the bay and entering the Temburong river was a completely new adventure for Manisah and her friends. She thought how funny it was that all her life, she had never been to this district before. She wondered about how closed and protected her life had been. She knew from that moment onwards, she had to spend more time travelling and visiting new places. Manisah did not want to be - as the local proverb goes - 'the frog that lives under the coconut shell'. She could see in the eyes of her friends, that they felt the same way too. They were merely visiting another district, but it felt like a journey to a new country!

Once reaching Bangar town, Manisah's group realised they were not alone. There were other groups, around 100 eager boisterous young men and women. The contingent got herded into buses and travelled to the adventure learning centre. This was a chance for introductions and make new acquaintances, especially with the opposite sex. The buses were not air-conditioned, compounding the sweltering heat, but this did nothing to dampen the mood and the chatter amongst the participants. What an exciting time! No more worries and no more reservations. There were instances of flirtations and the show-offs had their captive audience to entertain.

Eventually, they reached the training center built just above the riverbanks of the fast flowing Temburong river. The entire compound was within the confines of a real tropical rainforest. There was a two-storey main building construct made of hardwood. Its design was meant to follow the contours of the steep sloped site. This main building was facing the shallow but fast flowing river.

Manisah could see small rocks in the river, and the small whitewash reaffirming the shape of the smooth rocks. Gigantic jungle trees towered around the site, protecting the area from the harsh equatorial sun. There was a simple rope suspension bridge that went across the river to a grassy clearing field on a higher ground opposite the main building. Manisah wondered about the purpose of the rope bridge, and why was there a clearing up there. The place was surreal and beautiful. As she breathed in the fresh cool jungle air, she reminded herself that she was here for 4 days and she was going to make the best out of it.

The contingent was split into smaller groups and ushered into their orientation of the site. Each group had a specific site instructor and they had to nominate a team leader from amongst them.

A male nursing student; Max, was nominated as Manisah's group leader. He actually had a very long name. Somehow in university, he decided he wanted to be called Max because it sounded glamorous and more importantly, it sounded like he could be in charge, and hence he was in-charge of most university projects.

That night they played all kinds of 'ice-breaking' games to help them get to know each other better. The group also took part in a series of team building mini-games till late night. Finally, they were assigned segregated sleeping quarters in the main building. As Manisah laid in bed, she recited a prayer and appreciated the chorus of frogs, insects and assumed friendly nocturnal jungle creatures that lullabied her to sleep.

The very next day, the groups were woken up early in the morning and after prayers, they had a hearty breakfast. They had a big day to look forward to and the day was filled with many indoor team building activities. Later in the afternoon, everybody took turns in a river floating activity where each person was to wear a lifejacket, lie on their backs in the water and float down the river to a designated spot.

The water was actually cold, and as much as she tried her best not to sip the clear river water, she could taste how refreshing the stream was. Of course, as a future nurse, she knew there were unseen dangers in drinking untreated river water, no matter how clean it looked. As she floated gently down the river, Manisah closed her eyes as she let the light streaming thru the tree canopy warmly caress her face. Just as she began to really enjoy the experience, the warmth disappeared without warning, and a deep cold sensation enveloped her face.

Manisah opened her eyes and noticed how dark it had suddenly become. The water became frigid cold. She turned to her side and stood up. The river was only knee-deep. She saw her other friends still enjoying their river-floating experience. Before she could call out to her friends, she saw there was a womanly figure on the riverbank. The woman was looking directly at her. Manisah squinted but before she could focus her eyes, droplets of water streamed down from her hair to her eyes. She wiped them and when she opened her eyes again, she saw there was no one on the riverbank. She started to shiver in fear. Manisah convinced herself that she must have imagined it. This was daytime after all. She convinced herself that spirits only appear at night and doubted herself. Do they ever appear in the daytime?

She got out of the stream and sat on her own near the main building. She tried to convince herself that it was the effect of looking directly at the sunlight passing thru the tree canopy. Her mind was full of so many unanswered questions.

"You seem to be quieter than your usual self, Manisah," Max sat next to her. She was surprised he remembered her name. Manisah tried to muster a smile, she wanted to say something but ended up lost in her own thoughts, and hence lost for words.

"I know the stream is a bit cold, let's grab some hot tea and warm ourselves up," Max grabbed her hand, and she did nothing to resist. They went to the refreshments table and made themselves some hot tea. Chatting to Max, she quickly forgot about the river incident. It was at this moment, she realised Max was beyond a bubbly personality; he was truly uplifting.

The day went by quickly and their evening was filled with more team building games. The next day, the groups were told that they had to cross the rope suspension bridge across the river.

Walking on the simple suspension bridge was a frightening experience for the un-initiated. The most eccentric thing was that they had to wear a lifejacket when crossing this bridge. The instructors kept mentioning about an incident by which one of the participants had fallen off the rope bridge and nearly drowned. After that, everyone had to wear a lifejacket when crossing the bridge. There was also a whistle-blowing protocol when crossing.

Once they reached the other side of the bridge, everyone could see the grassy clearing and what laid beyond it. At the edge of the clearings, there were several wall-less stilted huts.

Everyone was whispering, "We're going to be sleeping there on the third evening, which is tonight!"

There were no walls which meant they would be sleeping more or less out in the open and exposed to the jungle environment.

Before anyone could debate the risks and benefits of sleeping there, the instructors had set them on a path to a hill called the 'ant hill'. It was a hike into the jungle. They filed in pairs and trekked through the jungle. Halfway there, Manisah and her friend noticed there was a jungle track on their right that was flanked on both sides with the most beautiful small white flowers. No one else had commented about it. The two girls were truly enticed to explore this track. Manisah's heart started pounding wildly. Every instinct within her told her that this was a mistake. She and her friend should not go through here, but the temptation was too great. It was as though they had no control over their bodies. They both took a few steps towards the mystical white flower track.

"Manisah! Naimah! What do you think you're doing?" It was Max's loud voice. As though breaking a spell, the two girls stopped in their tracks, and moved no further.

"Come back here, and make sure you guys stay with the group!" Max reaffirmed, as the duo realised the deviant track there were about to wander off to had no white flowers, let alone any flowers flanking the track.

"Max, I don't know what happened…" Manisah tried to explain but Max gestured for them not to talk anymore. They understood this was not the time and place to talk about what had happened. Manisah kept quiet and kept close to Max for the rest of their trek to 'Ant Hill'. She kept wondering what would have happened if Max hadn't stopped them. She could feel unseen eyes watching her every move. The jungle had suddenly become so dangerous.

Whilst the rest of the group were amazed and awed by the view at 'Ant Hill', Manisah and her friend Naimah felt particularly lost and anxious. They both felt an urgency to get back to the main building and sleep it off.

However, after returning from 'Ant Hill', their group had to pack their essentials and prepare for a night at the open-air stilted huts on the other side of the river. Everyone was going to be sleeping together on the floor of the stilted open-air huts. Their sleeping bags would be the only protection they have against the elements.

Once inside the hut, Manisah noticed a thin rope running across one wooden pillar to the other. This was on the side that was facing the jungle. Their group instructor advised everyone not to touch or untie the rope. One of the participants asked why, and the instructor merely placed her index finger on her lips. Some things are best not to be talked about here. Someone mentioned it must be some sort of 'Guris' or protection rope against evil spirits, whilst another got upset because they were not supposed to talk about it in the first place for fear of 'cabul' or jinxing.

When it was time to sleep, they had to switch off all their flashlights. It had become intensely dark all around. Manisah saw tall shadows running around in the dark jungle, she did her best to ignore it and focused on the beautiful stars that littered the night sky. She watched all her friends fall asleep.

She closed her eyes and tried to doze off, but her heart was pounding and her breath became shallow and faster. She could hear a very loud rumble in the jungle, the sound of a hundred giant creatures stomping through the jungle, and yet it woke no one else up. Manisah uttered a prayer and kept praying for protection. Eventually, to Manisah's relief, the rumble died down and Manisah counted her blessings and yet she could not sleep. She looked at her digital watch and saw it was already 1am.

She could hear the sound of a motorboat speeding up the river. She wondered if it was one of the other instructors. She had a deep thought about it and became very alarmed. No boat would be travelling at 1am let alone at night in the shallow river here. She could hear footsteps heading towards the hut. It sounded like an army heading towards the tent. It did not make sense to her.

Seeing that none of her friends or instructors had woken up, Manisah pulled her sleeping bag over her head and curled tightly. It was getting hotter and Manisah was sweating furiously. She dared not pop her head to see what was happening. The sound of footsteps was nearby and fast, as though the 'people' were jogging on the same spot. Staccato. Light fast steps. She could tell it was by their hut. The sound was coming from the four sides of the hut. Manisah and her group were surrounded! She could not hold it anymore, she wanted to scream for help. Fear gripped her neck, if she screamed, surely; she would be dragged into the jungle by these 'people'.

A loud piercing scream shattered everything. Manisah jumped out of her sleeping bag and onto her feet. She switched on her flashlight and she was ready to hit whatever was going to abduct her. Voices came from all around her, groans and questions. A few of her friends had gotten up to find out who had screamed. It was not Manisah. Her friend Naimah was seemingly having a bad nightmare. Naimah had screamed and was struggling to wake up. It took a few of the instructors to wake her up and calm her down. Naimah asked if she could go back home immediately and the instructor had to carefully explain that it would be impossible, given their remote location. Eventually, Naimah calmed down and went to sleep without any further incident. Their instructor did a quick roll call and everyone was accounted for. Manisah felt a sense of relief that no one had been abducted. After that she too fell asleep quickly.

When the morning sun came and everyone had woken up, the instructor noticed that there was a towel on the rope. The instructor was very unpleased asking whose towel it was. It was Naimah's towel. As much as the instructor wanted to berate Naimah, she decided to hold back.

Later on, everyone had packed up and was heading back to the main building. Manisah noticed the instructor stayed back at the hut to untie the rope. She was uttering something and then went on to re-tie the rope.

Manisah made sure she was the last to leave the area.

When the instructor caught up to Manisah, she took the courage to tell the instructor about the sound of footsteps around their hut the night before.

Her instructor shrugged and said it was one of the other instructors who was making a night patrol. The bead of sweat that went down the instructor's forehead betrayed her lie. Manisah decided not to pursue questions that were unwilling to be answered. She was going back home today. After all, what happens in Temburong should stay in Temburong.

The Nocturnal

It is strange that when I share about poltergeist sightings and experiences at Jalan Kebangsaan Lama or Kebangsaan Lama Road area, I often get a number of people who have their own experiences to share. This is Yusof's story.

In 1981, my parents had bought their first house at 'Jalan Kebangsaan Lama' or Kebangsaan Lama Road. My parents were overjoyed and zealously proud, as it was deemed as an important milestone achievement for citizens, who are second generation Chinese, to own property. No one could say we were not of this land, not of this beautiful country anymore. Even though I did end up working in the construction industry, I never quite understood this until my wife and I bought our own house together.

Our 'new' house was a large house on a large piece of land, as per most 'modern' houses back then in the 1980s. Everything was per the trend back then, the rooms were spacious and had horizontal window pane shutters that creaked loudly every time you open and close it. Sometimes, you would wonder if the window panes would break when you open the windows too fast. Downstairs, the windows had cast-iron security grille installed as an anti-burglar deterrent. My parents allocated one of the upstairs rooms for me. I was glad to finally have my own room and not have to share with my brother.

Everyone was very excited about settling down in the house and had not notice the strange occurrences at home.

It all began one evening in 1988, or at least that was when I first noticed it. I was never a superstitious child and I used to never believe in any supernatural entities. I had been staying up late at night to study and prepare for my 'BJCE' exams (now this has been changed to the Year 8 'SPE' exam). The window shutters in my room would rattle from time to time. I thought it was the vibrations from the window air-conditioner. Initially, I thought nothing of it. The windows rattled on and off until early morning. The next day, the same thing had reoccurred. And again, the following day. It came to a point where I got quite annoyed, so I switched off the air-con and hit the books again.

A few minutes later, the sound was there again. It was much louder. This time, it sounded more like something hard and sharp was tapping on the glass panes. I wondered if it was a woodpecker bird, but I was sure these birds sleep at night. I went to the window and looked out. There was no sign of any birds. I opened the shutters to peek out and saw nothing. Although I saw nothing, I felt as though someone was looking back at me. It was a silly feeling and I really could not justify it.

This happened on other nights. It got me quite riled up, especially whenever I drew the curtains, the tapping would start immediately. Sometimes I would switch off the lights in the room and peeked out from the corner to catch that 'culprit bird'.

On other evenings, I would check the shutters and the mechanisms to see if there was anything loose or stuck. Perhaps this was how I ended up in the construction industry in the first place. On other occasions, I would open and slam the shutters just to shoo off the birds. Even though I had not seen any sign that it was a bird, I had set in conclusion that it was some sort of a persistent nocturnal bird.

As the day for the exams got closer, I thought it would be better if I study in a different room, away from potential distractions. I was in my parents' bedroom and to my surprise, the window tapping started there too. It must be following me! The windows in my parents' bedroom had been upgraded to the modern sliding windows. I was livid. I grabbed a torch light and slid open the windows. Staring out, I saw nothing but the pitch-black darkness. The jungle was near to our house and yet it was strangely very dead quiet. Despite this, I had the same strange feeling that someone was watching me, hiding in the darkness. When I told my mum about it, she concluded that it must have been a bird or a monkey.

After that, I simply used my headphones and cranked up

the volume when studying. Surprisingly listening to rock music really helped me with my studies. Anyway, I eventually went abroad to study civil engineering at university. After graduating, I returned home. The house still looked the same except all the windows had now been upgraded to sliding windows. This was better for keeping the air-conditioned rooms cold.

Can you imagine my surprise and annoyance when the damned tapping noise happened again? After all these years of peaceful nights elsewhere, this had to happen in my own room! When the tapping started, I opened the window and there was nothing outside. I heard no fluttering of wings or any other noise. A void of any sound and I had that same feeling that someone or something was watching. In some ways, I was glad that my job at that time meant that I was sleeping overnight at my workplace instead. Anyway, I moved out of that room to another room on the ground floor, and I had no window tapping incident, or at the very least, I had never noticed it.

Several years later, when I had gotten married, my sister moved into my old room along with her children. It was the second biggest bedroom in the house, so it made sense for them. Sometimes, our Indonesian maid would be there to help put the children to sleep.

One evening, the Indonesian maid, who claimed to be gifted, ran out of the room, shuddering in fear. Something had spooked her. She heard the tapping on the windows, which was exactly the same experience I had when I was a teenager, except that she could see a 'Pontianak' dressed in a blood-stained white gown, hovering in mid-air whilst tapping on the glass windows with her sharp long fingernails! The Pontianak had long black hair which went down below her feet. She had blood-dripping red eyes and her face was pale white. She had an evil grin as she stared intently at the maid. The maid was at first frozen in fear. When the Pontianak gestured with her finger to come closer, the maid ran away from the window and out of the room.

She had also seen that the backyard was filled with 'orang - orang halus' or the 'invisible' spirits. The 'orang-orang halus' had made a house in one of the trees whilst there was a separate entity, a tall dark spirit living in a separate 'belimbing' or starfruit tree. She kept reciting prayers hoping to discourage them from disturbing the household.

However, my sister and her children would; from time to time, hear the same window tapping. They did their best to ignore it, as they reckoned it posed no danger to them. I no longer stay in that house and as for the rest of my family, they had no other supernatural encounters.

Dr. Aammton Alias

The Night Watchman

Aswadi had been a security guard for many years. He was 30 years old and had been working at various facilities in the Tutong district. His transfer to the Sungai Basong Recreational Park was quite sudden. It was his first time working at a recreational park. He was told to fill an unexpected vacancy as the previous elderly security guard had passed away. Aswadi did not mind as it meant the commute to work was nearer and he assumed the job would be 'less risky' and less demanding than being a security guard at a water plant for example.

Aswadi had been to the Sungai Basong recreational park several times though during leisure time and this was during the occasional afternoons. He was expected to work the night shifts there. His boss told him not to worry that although he was the lone security guard there, he should be able to have ample sleep time. All he had to do was to make sure he had his mobile phone and walkie-talkie radio with him at all times and to respond to it, in cases of emergencies. This was unlikely to happen as the park was closed at night.

Aswadi started his first shift late in the afternoon. His day-shift colleague could not wait to go home, eagerly passing him the walkie-talkie radio and designated mobile phone, and then going through the motions and emergency contact details. After that, Aswadi made his pre-dusk round which was a good flat circuit walk around the park. He watched the various people jogging and walking pass by. Most were in their sports gear whilst a few were still wearing their work clothes and had only changed their work shoes to sports shoes. Some walked with their spouses or boyfriends and girlfriends, whilst a few others brought along their children. Everyone had to squeeze in their exercise time in their busy daily lives. There were also a few cyclists including children who brought their bicycles with training wheels. Most cyclists in the district would prefer to join the numerous cycling groups who cycled on the main roads and highway - complete with escort cars. Aswadi took notice of the rollerblading 'couples' who appreciated the smooth asphalt and cement pathways to lap through circuits. He wished he could have moments like that but time seemed to have passed by with nothing but lost opportunities and bitter memories.

Aswadi always smiled as he made his round, and when eyes met or smiles were exchanged, he would nod subtly. It was a professional habit he had developed, a means to acknowledge the other person and assure that everything is fine. He had no need to be suspicious of anyone as everyone here were good people.

By sunset, he had a cigarette break at the security guard shed. With nothing else to do, he would check his mobile phone, and have long chats in the various WhatsApp chat groups he was involved in.

Now it was dark, the streetlights and the pavement lights lit the park and its surrounding area. It was quiet and serene at the same time. This would be an easy job for him as he was simply the night watchman of an empty park.

Aswadi had mastered the art of using up the vacant time he had. He had been introduced to a young 24-year-old divorcee named Alia. Alia had 2 young toddlers from her previous marriage, which had ended violently.

Aswadi had developed a liking towards her. However, he was cautious of committing to relationships where children were involved, and an ex-husband who was in jail for domestic violence.

He needed more time to get to know her. She had a sweet raspy voice, and hence he would spend much time talking to her on the phone.

He noticed that there was poor mobile phone reception in the security shed so he had to step out to make his phone call. He would smoke whilst he whispered sweet nothings to her and when he got excited, he would laugh raucously.

At first, Aswadi began to notice the strange shapes forming in the shadows, which he realised were shadow-like figures running in between the streetlights. He had been accustomed to such sightings when he was alone. No matter how many times he said he was used to it, his body was clearly not and had always responded with goosebumps.

Aswadi talked louder on his phone. He was determined to ignore the distractions as he was getting on a good vibe with Alia.

Then it began to escalate. There was a loud rustling sound around him. This made no sense to him as the night was windless. His instincts pointed towards a supernatural presence but Aswadi was even more determined to ignore it. Eventually, the sound disappeared and Aswadi sighed in relief.

Just when he thought it was over, a deep croaky voice whispered loudly to his right ear, "Quiet!". He could feel cold damp air rushing towards his right ear. Aswadi was startled and jumped in reflex, dropping his mobile phone on the ground. He picked up his phone and hurried back into the security shed. He was truly spooked. He had previously had supernatural encounters before, but he had never heard a voice so clear and so close to his ear.

He glanced at his Casio digital watch; it was half-past midnight. He recited a prayer mantra and decided he should stay in the shed. His mobile phone rang again, it was Alia. With her voice on the line, he quickly forgot about the poltergeist whisperer. His mood was elated as they shared their school childhood memories. Aswadi realised he had so much in common with Alia and wondered if it was a 'simple' matter of age difference and time that had kept them apart from each other until now.

He wished he had not been interrupted. In the corner of his eyes, he caught a glimpse of several pairs of legs dangling from the trees. Their feet had no shoes and were not moving at all, except the gentle and slow swaying motion of the entire bodies. Lifeless. He could not ignore it, so he glanced up and saw 'people' hanging with ropes around their necks. He could see the glint of their popped-out eyes in the dim sodium orange light, their vacant stares and tongues stuck out fixed by jaw rigor mortis.

Aswadi dropped down to the ground, shocked by what he had seen. He gasped and shone his flashlight at the tree branches. There were no ropes or corpses hanging from its branches. It was the trick of the eye, he thought.

He thought it was best not to tempt fate or whatever it was that he was upsetting. He typed a message to Alia telling her that he had to go and carry out a routine patrol. He then switched off his phone and stayed put in the security shed until the sunrise.

The next evening, he had almost forgotten about his previous night's ordeal, and once again found himself talking to his more-than-a-friend Alia. So far nothing had happened. Taking a cigarette break whilst charging his mobile phone to his power-bank, he looked at his watch and noticed it was already nearly 1am. Aswadi was about to make another call on his phone when without warning, there was a loud smack on his face. He had been slapped so hard to a point he lost his balance and fell.

He got back up on his feet, ready to confront his assailant but found himself alone. There was not a sign of anyone there. He concluded very quickly; he must have been slapped by an evil spirit. Aswadi panicked and ran away from the park. He speedily drove back home and once things had settled enough; he texted a message to his supervisor to let him know that he quit his job.

The next day, his boss or supervisor asked him to come to the office for a quick chat. His boss begged him not to quit his job, not at least until they can get a replacement. Aswadi was prone to emotional blackmail. Even though his boss was actually a tough guy, seeing him plead to Aswadi made it difficult to quit his job.

So that night, he found himself working at the park again. He did his best not to use his mobile phone except to type the occasional messages. Alia called him as she was worried why he didn't seem as cordial as before. He had to answer the phone call; he did not want to lose the good relationship that was building between them. The moment he greeted her, he was slapped hard on the face. Again, there was no sign of his attacker. Scared and furious, Aswadi left the park that very night and quit his job, for the second time.

The funny thing was that a few days later, he was convinced to work again at the same park. His supervisor had a spiritual adviser to bless his shed and advised him on prayers before work. He was eventually able to explain to Alia what had happened, which was a good excuse for Alia (accompanied by her younger brother) to visit him at work during his night shift. A week or two later, it was decided that there should be two security guards assigned for night duties at the park. This way, Aswadi was not all alone at the park. Since then, Aswadi still had the occasional encounter of sightings and strange noises in the middle of the night. The good thing was that he did not have any further physical supernatural encounters.

Toto's Confrontation

Syifa; a 9-year-old girl, has been living in England for the past few years, whilst her mother, an orthopedic surgeon was completing her specialist training in the United Kingdom. This is her story.

***

It was strange to come back home again. Even though we visited our home country for the holidays, there was nothing like coming home and knowing we were here to stay. Our house in Jerudong had been vacant most of the time. Its only visitors were my grandmother and my uncles who would check on the house and clean the house from time to time.

I never thought one could be a stranger to one's own house, and yet that was what it had been. There was an uneasy feeling when we stayed the first night at home. It made little sense as we should be overjoyed by the thought of being back for good. I told my mom it was like we had moved into someone else's house and we weren't welcome. My mom was a bit spooked out about it, but none of us had seen or experienced anything else. She reasoned that perhaps we were simply used to our own place in the UK. It was then I realised that I did miss what I had in England: my school friends, the usual

189

creature comforts and my routine habits.

Mom said sometimes it is hard to accept change, but everyone goes through it. Being a doctor, she had to give it a diagnosis or at least a name: adjustment issues. I don't like it when she does that. I guess that's what doctors do; they have to give things labels - make life and people easier to organise; I think. She reminded me that the only constant in life is change. She asked me to remember her words and think about it from time to time.

I did my best to accept what Mom had said, but I could not help from noticing that occasionally when I was alone, the shadows in the corner seem to be longer, seem to be more playful. Sometimes in the corner of my eyes, I would catch a glimpse of the shadows moving away as though trying to catch me. At times, when I was in my room, it would feel as though someone was there with me, someone I could not see. I would get goosebumps all over my body or it would suddenly feel chilly in the warm room. I tried to convince myself that it was simply a matter of 'adjustment'. If only there was a medicine I could take.

Instead of medicine, a saviour had come to rescue my family and me. We had a new visitor. A stray cat had decided to move into our house compound and had a liking towards me. It was a grey adult cat and for a stray cat it seemed well-groomed. Its gray fur was thick and yet soft to touch. There was a pattern on its fur that acknowledged this cat must be related to clouded leopards, jaguars and tigers.

My parents were initially not too keen for us to have a house cat especially since it was a stray cat, but I begged and put on my best 'sulk-face' and as I had predicted they caved in. I took it to the vet to have it checked and vaccinated.

My elder sister, Syasya, was the one who decided the name of the cat. She named him Tobias, and that somehow changed to Toto. Toto was a shorter name, and much easier to pronounce. Everyone in the house agreed and even the cat seemed to agree to his new name. I brought Toto to our bedroom - I shared my bedroom with my sister - and found a special mat for it. Sometimes, he would sneak in and jump onto a corner of our bed. He would sleep there till the morning. I felt safe.

Somehow, I felt it was as though the cat was watching over and protecting us from evil. Although, I had no justification for this thought, somehow, I knew deep within myself that this was the truth. Sometimes I thought this was a silly thing to think about, I would say to myself that I had watched too many adventure movies. That would be what Mom would say!

One late evening, just before bedtime, my mom and I were reciting several Holy Verses from the Holy Book, when suddenly and without warning, Toto had jumped onto the bed and started hissing and growling. His fur had puffed up, his tail upright and the fur on that tail was puffed up too. His face snarled, revealing his sharp teeth and his claws revealed all its nails. His body posture was poised, ready to jump and attack, and kill if necessary. I had never seen Toto like this before. He looked very different to the cute docile cat I knew. He looked ready for battle, the fight of his life. Yet, we could not see his enemy. He was staring at the wall behind the headboard of our bed.

We thought maybe he had seen a lizard or something similar, so we peeked behind the headboard. However, there was nothing there. Toto's eyes were wide and there was a glint in his eyes. No matter what we did to calm him down, he did not budge; he did not stop growling.

The more I stared at the wall, the more I could see that it was not all empty. There was seemingly a transparent pattern moving there. It was not at all clear, like a tear in the fabric of our universe. My heart was pounding hard, my breathing fast and shallow and my body was getting colder. Intuitively, I stepped away from Toto and held onto my mom. She too held me tight, ensuring her body was shielding mine.

We both sensed it at the same time. There was something there, almost invisible to our eyes, but not to Toto's eyes. Whatever it was, Toto could see it as bright as day. We knew in our hearts, whatever it was, it did not have good intentions. I wanted to take Toto out of harm's way but before I could do that my mom dragged me out of the room. We hurried to our dad and told him what had happened. Dad jumped on his feet and brought us back to my bedroom. There, we noticed Toto was looking much calmer, no longer growling, but his fur was still puffed up. His pose was still the same but less intense. He had the same killer look and still stared at the wall.

The whole family continued reciting the Holy Verses and when we noticed Toto had jumped off the bed and switched back to his 'docile mode', Dad thought whatever confrontation Toto had, had now been resolved. Toto slept with me that night. Someone once told me that Toto is actually the name of a dog in the book (and movie) titled The Wonderful Wizard of Oz. I would smile silently because I realised that whilst others may have guard dogs, I have a brave guard cat.

------The End------

"The real horror

and

monster

is actually us.

Driven by our greed

and our selfishness,

we have become

destroyer of worlds…"

Aammton Alias

About The Author

Dr. Aammton Alias has been a family physician for almost two decades. Currently, he practices at a private community clinic.

He is the Vice-President of RELA (REading and Literacy Association). One of the many goals of this organisation is to strive for every child to own and cherish at least one book.

He is a keen conservationist and environmentalist who is deeply concerned with the state of the world the next generation will inherit.

You can reach him via:

http://www.about.me/aammton
Twitter: @Aammton
Telegram: @ElTonyX
Instagram: @aammton
Facebook Page: www.fb.me/aammtonalias

What Happens After This?

Now that you have read the book, you might be wondering what happens next. You can always reach me on my Facebook page, Instagram or Telegram especially if you have a ghost story to share or you are simply curious on when my next book is coming out.

I have written eBooks and there is a 'universal book link' for the Real Ghost Stories of Borneo 3.

https://books2read.com/rgsob3

This way you can check which eBook platform it is currently available on.

You can also follow me at:

www.ap.aammton.com

https://books2read.com/author/aammton-alias/subscribe/23128/

or

b2rsub.aammton.com

My Other Books

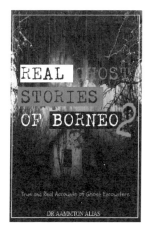

If you enjoyed this book, then you definitely would enjoy reading Real Ghost Stories of Borneo book 1 and book 2.

Both books are collections of accounts of real ghost encounters, written by a family physician working in Borneo.

These supernatural tales are true accounts with a unique insight into the local population and what ails them. Be warned, very few of these stories have a 'happily ever after' ending.

A number of these stories may appear to have been left open ended with no explanation, as had been shared with the author in that manner.

www.ghost1.b1percent.com

www.ghost2.b1percent.com

Please note **True Ghost Stories of Borneo** is a US Amazon version of the same book.

Killing Dreams

This is the second book in the series: The Bunian Conspiracy. Originally inspired by the mysterious events in the jungles of Borneo island, Killing Dreams, a supernatural fantasy thriller uncovers the events in the aftermath of the horrific 3rd December Ingei jungle 'incident' . Captain Sarin and his elite recon unit, the Prowling Tigers, are deep in Borneo's Ingei jungle tasked to investigate the gruesome massacre of the expedition team and more importantly, to find the unaccounted.

www.kill.b1percent.com

The Last Bastion of Ingei: Imminent

On the mysterious island of Borneo, three conservationists work together, battling against the odds. Their mission, to stop poachers from exploiting the endangered wildlife from being hunted and sold, key amongst them, the prized, enigmatic and rare 'Pangolin'. However, they are themselves being stalked by a far greater menace than they could ever imagine. The jungle hides its secret well, but the friends are about to confront an ancient menace, far older than humanity itself, an old foe long since forgotten. Soon, the fate of Mankind will hang in the balance. Meanwhile, a captain in the elite 5th Recon Unit is brought back to face an unspoken tragedy that no one believes happened, whilst elsewhere, recent supernatural events re-activate a secretive vanguard for human salvation: The LIMA

www.ingei.b1percent.com

Be The One Percent: Unlock Secrets to True Success, Real Wealth & Ultimate Happiness

www.book.b1percent.com

The King And The Minister

www.king.b1percent.com

The Vessel of Our Writing Dreams: Where Do Our Ideas Come From

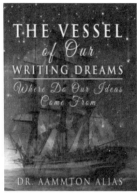

www.vessel.b1percent.com

LET ME GO! How to Get Off Unwanted WhatsApp Chat Groups For Good

www.wtfrak.b1percent.com

Now Everyone Can Write & Publish A Book In 3 Days

www.write.b1percent.com

How I Became a Self-Published Author:
The Journey to 51,000 Word

Published by MPH:
www.mph1.b1percent.com